THE ALPHABETICAL HOOKUP

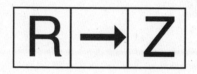

Phoebe McPhee

POCKET BOOKS
New York   London   Toronto   Sydney   Singapore

This book is a work of fiction. Names, characters, places, and incidents are products of the author's imagination or are used fictitiously. Any resemblance to actual events or locales or persons, living or dead, is entirely coincidental.

An *Original* Publication of MTV Books/Pocket Books

POCKET BOOKS, a division of Simon & Schuster Inc.
1230 Avenue of the Americas, New York, NY 10020

Copyright © 2002 by 17th Street Productions, an Alloy, Inc. company and One Ear Productions

 Produced by 17th Street Productions,
an Alloy, Inc. company
151 West 26th Street
New York, NY 10001

MTV Music Television and all related titles, logos, and characters are trademarks of MTV Networks, a division of Viacom International Inc.

ISBN: 0-7434-4844-8

First MTV Books/Pocket Books trade paperback printing September 2002

10 9 8 7 6 5 4 3 2 1

POCKET and colophon are registered trademarks of Simon & Schuster Inc.

Cover design by Amy Beadle
Printed in the U.S.A.

For information regarding special discounts for bulk purchases, please contact Simon & Schuster Special Sales at 1-800-456-6798 or business@simonandschuster.com

Celeste Alexander had just had the worst nightmare of her entire life. In the dream she was lying on a giant roulette wheel that wouldn't stop spinning, and she couldn't get off it. No matter how much she screamed, the wheel just wouldn't stop. It was like some twisted episode of *Wheel of Fortune* meets *Casino.* Grotesque men stood around screaming letters of the alphabet at her while she spun completely out of control.

Celeste blinked a couple of times, then sat up in bed as the events of the night before slowly came back to her. Casino Night. That had been real, and it hadn't been a nightmare at all. She and her roommates, Jodi and Ali, had won back all the money they needed. The money that would keep Ali from getting thrown out of Pollard University.

It had been a really close call. They had been incredibly lucky, and they'd had an amazing time last night. But Celeste was still sure of one thing: She had to quit the Alphabetical Hookup List.

She was also sure of one other thing: She needed the

strongest hangover medicine she could get her hands on.

She slowly hobbled out of bed and made it to her dresser, yanking open the drawer that held a neatly ordered collection of extra-strength Excedrin packets, No-Doz, pens and highlighters, stamps, a mug, Earl Grey tea bags, Twizzlers, and an AT&T prepaid calling card.

Celeste grabbed an Excedrin packet, suffering a very unpleasant flashback to the last time she'd used one from this stash—the morning after she had lost her virginity to the scummiest creature on the planet, Buster Needham, who happened to be her roommate Jodi's ex-boyfriend. It had been the first in a long string of humiliations she had recently lived through, all because of this crazy game she and Jodi and Ali were playing, racing to be the first to kiss a guy for every letter of the alphabet—in alphabetical order.

Celeste looked around for something to wash down the Excedrin with since the thought of going out the door, down the hall, and down one flight of stairs to the soda machine made her feel like she was right back on the roulette wheel in her dream. She spotted some old chocolate Slim-Fast shakes on the floor by her dresser and cracked one open. Celeste had bought the Slim-Fast shakes after she, Jodi, and Ali had made the mistake of weighing themselves a month into the semester. She had stopped drinking them because after she drank one, they would invariably order a pizza and she would eat two and a half slices, anyway.

She looked at her roommates sound asleep in their beds and smiled, thinking about how much she had, well, hated them when she first met them. Jodi Stein. A Long Island jock/goddess with big hair who still called her father "Daddy." Pre-Pollard Celeste would haven taken one look at Jodi and written her off instantly as your typical brainless, superficial girl whose main goal in life was to join a sorority. And actually, Jodi *had* come to college convinced she was going to pledge Kappa Kappa Gamma.[1] But after getting to know her better, Celeste had realized that Jodi was incredibly fun to hang out with and, more importantly, along with the big hair, Jodi also had a really big heart.

And then there was Ali Sheppard, the girl from Atlanta who had a nose ring and a propensity for pigtails and some-times wore pants made out of strange materials. Ali had about fifty million interests, and at first Celeste had thought Ali was as flaky as Jib and Carla.[2] And yeah, Ali *wasn't* the most focused person in the world. In fact, she was basically flunking out of college. But the more Celeste hung around her, the more she realized that Ali was fiercely loyal and ridiculously funny. And after a while she even got used to the fact that Ali called everyone, even Celeste, "dude."

Celeste finished the last sip of her Slim-Fast, put her head down on her desk, and waited for the Excedrin to take effect. After a few minutes she heard a rustling noise from Ali's bed.

"Oh, dude," Ali groaned. "Did one of you put a dirty sock in my mouth while I slept? Because that's what it feels like."

1 Due to an incident involving the sorority president's hair and some pink vomit, Jodi was not invited to pledge.

2 Celeste's parents, Jib and Carla, insist she use their first names.

Jodi let out a low moan. "Please don't talk so loud," she mumbled. "You're going to break my head open."

Celeste looked back and forth between her hungover roommates, wondering if now was the right time to make her announcement. Well, it was probably as good as any. "I'm quitting the AHUL," she said. "I'm pulling out of the contest. I've made up my mind, so don't try to talk me out of it. But don't worry, I'll still pay up at the end and help take the winner on a night out in Atlanta."

"Wait, what? You can't quit *now,*" Jodi said, suddenly wide awake. "We're all more than halfway through the alphabet."

Celeste cringed. "Actually, not all of us," she said. As long as she was making statements that would piss off her roommates, she might as well throw this one into the mix. "I cheated," she announced. "I made up all those guys I said I kissed . . . including Professor McKean. He never kissed me. I'm really only up to *D.* Well, I mean, I kissed a *D.* So I'm up to *E.*"

Ali and Jodi exchanged looks of shock. Then Ali started to smile. "Dude, now you *really* can't quit the list," she said. She sat up in bed, pushing the covers off. "I mean, since when has Celeste Alexander cheated at *anything?* The AHUL is turning you into a whole new . . . well, you!"

Celeste couldn't believe Ali wasn't mad, but then she saw that Jodi was frowning. "I kind of wish you hadn't lied to us," Jodi said.

Celeste felt her heart squeeze. "I know, I'm so sorry," she said. "I shouldn't have lied. And that's why I'm telling you the truth now—I have to stop. I have to quit the list."

"Jodi's right, you shouldn't have lied to us," Ali said. "But come on, don't you see how good the AHUL is for you? You're finally learning how to take a few risks, live on the edge a little. And things are going so well. I mean, I actually got my *Q* and everything! And since we won back my tuition last night, I don't even have to stress about money anymore. It's a clearly a good omen. And what about the fact that you both kissed someone with a guitar tattoo who had the exact initials you needed? That's like fate or something telling us the AHUL is the right thing to do. Come on, Celeste, this is what bonds us. It's like if one of the Three Musketeers just quit and Don Juan or Don Quixote or whoever that dude was got stuck with just two of them."

"What are you talking about?" Celeste said. "Obviously you haven't even read *The Three Musketeers.* Or *Don Quixote.*"

"I saw *The Three Amigos,*" Ali said. "Anyway, you can't quit. It wouldn't be fair."

Celeste frowned. She didn't want to let down her friends, but for the most part the AHUL had just brought her bad luck and misery. She needed to take herself out of the game for a while—figuratively and literally.

"It just isn't fun for me," Celeste explained, plopping back down on her bed. "And honestly, the guitar-tattoo thing just freaks me out. How could that be possible? It seemed like it had to be the same guy, but that doesn't make any sense. But then how could two guys be so similar, but one's named David and one's named Lucas? Something's weird with that, don't you think?"

Ali thought about the guitar-tattooed guy *she'd* seen at the bar, Dimers, who'd said his name was Mark. She hadn't told Jodi and Celeste that the night before, when they were talking about Lucas and David. It was pretty weird, but it couldn't have been the same guy, with three different names.

"I was thinking about that," Ali said. "It's probably just a popular tattoo at some local tattoo parlor or something. And come on, plenty of guys have brown hair, right?"

Celeste sighed. "Okay, I guess. But that's not the point, anyway. Maybe you two should consider putting an end to the list, too. Jodi, you're in love with Zack, and you might as well just face that. And Ali, you still have to start buckling down and studying. Otherwise you'll flunk out even if you *can* afford the tuition now. I don't know—maybe we should all take a little break, just until we can get a better grip on our lives."

Jodi and Ali listened solemnly to what Celeste was saying. Jodi got out of bed and knelt on the floor, then bent over and stretched her arms out as she rested in "Child's Pose," a yoga position that Zack had showed her when they were alone together in the library.

"Celeste has a point," Jodi said from the floor.

"Dude, are we supposed to have a conversation with you when you're kneeling on the floor with your ass sticking up in the air?" Ali asked Jodi.

"It helps my hangover," Jodi said.

"Dude, you've changed," Ali said. "You used to think a coffee milk shake was the best cure for a hangover, and now you're into this New Age yoga shit."

"Maybe we *should* quit," Jodi said. "I mean, in a way the list has fucked all of us up. I can definitely see the logic in quitting."

"That's probably because I'm winning," Ali said, shielding her eyes from the morning sun peeking in through the blinds. "As far as I'm concerned, the Alphabetical Hookup List has been the one bright light in an otherwise dark and dismal semester, and I'm not going to give that up."

"Yeah," Jodi said, sitting up. "And since Zack and I are really, truly over now—" She stopped herself in midsentence as the full weight of everything that had happened the night before hit her. Things had actually been going pretty well with Zack lately. There was the whole keeping her relationship with him a secret from her best friends problem and keeping the AHUL a secret from him—but mystery was supposed to make romance more exciting, anyway, right? But then, by some really fucking awful twist of fate, Zack had arrived at Casino Night just in time to see Jodi get her *L*.[3] She'd tried to explain that the kiss meant nothing, but Zack had freaked out and stormed off. Jodi felt her eyes tear up just thinking about it. She blinked rapidly, not wanting her friends to see her cry over Zack. "There's no better way to get over him than the AHUL," she said, her voice sounding a little less firm than she'd hoped. But she *would* get over Zack.

Unless . . . unless she didn't have to. Jodi bit her lip.

3 Who happened to be the guitar-tattoo-sporting guy named Lucas who matched the description of the guy named David, whom Celeste had kissed.

Like if she could track him down and see if maybe he'd cooled off and would give her another chance?

"Well, you two can go it alone, then," Celeste said. She took her Filofax out of her bag, tore out the AHUL page where she kept track of all three of their lists, and ripped it into tiny pieces.

It was like she was the first to leave *Survivor*. She hadn't had to eat rats, but she had kissed some really disgusting guys,[4] and now it was all for nothing. She was out of there. Her torch was extinguished. Her Alphabetical Hookup List was torn up.

Jodi and Ali didn't know what to say. They had both thought about quitting at one time or another, but the game was fun, and it was especially fun doing it together, and they had never wanted to quit for long. But Celeste seemed really serious.

They looked down at the torn pieces of paper on the floor. Scraps of letters and boys' names. They looked like paper Scrabble tiles that could be assembled to spell a whole word. Pieces of a weird puzzle. Both Jodi and Ali had the impulse to bend down and pick up all the pieces and keep them safe, but Celeste scooped them up unceremoniously and tossed them out the window. They blew off in all different directions. "Good-bye, boys," Celeste said.

There was something so sad about it—like in *Charlotte's Web* when Charlotte has all her baby spiders and they all fly away from her—but something hopeful, too.

□□□□□□□□□□□□□□□□□□□□□□□□□□□□□□□□□□

4 Andy the Bloated.

8

All Ali and Jodi knew was that things were somehow very different now.

"Well, Celeste, the door is always open if you change your mind and want to come back," Jodi said.

"Yeah, dude, you can always come back," Ali agreed.

Celeste nodded, but she knew she was going to stick to her decision. And Ali and Jodi were pretty sure she meant it, too, which just really, really sucked.

2

The vibe was kind of weird after Celeste made her announcement, so Jodi got up and dressed and went out, first in search of a coffee milk shake, because the yoga hadn't done a thing for her headache, and then in search of Zack.

She went to the Allween Library, all set to track down Zack and apologize for making a fool out of herself the night before. But just as she was about to enter the library, she stopped. It seemed to her that she was always in this position of finding Zack and apologizing to him. That was kind of weird, wasn't it? But the truth was she did keep doing stupid things where Zack was concerned, and last night had been the crème de la crème, the Academy Awards, the paramount peak of stupidity.

"Zack," she said out loud. She loved his name. She loved saying his name. It had been such a long time since she had liked a guy this much. The kind of like where she could spend an entire day in bed just thinking about him.

She and Ali and Celeste had gone on a crazy trip to Paris over Veteran's Day weekend, and all she had thought about the whole time was Zack. All the way over on the plane she had imagined that he was sitting in the seat next to her. Everywhere she went, she thought of little things she wanted to tell him, funny things she knew only he would get a kick out of, like when they had all put on this perfume in a little market in Paris and it turned out that the perfume was for dogs.

She hadn't felt that way about a guy since Buster. Or at least, since Buster in the old high school days when they were first going out. They had dated all through high school and then had come to PU together, and it had really been pretty great until he'd cheated on her. The weird thing was, she'd been she was right to end it. She didn't even miss Buster that much. She missed Zack.

Standing in front of Allween Library was kind of weird because it was where she had spent so much time with Zack. They had made out there one time. They were working together in the library as stackers, and everyone else had left, so they were alone and it was late at night, and they had just started kissing. And it was incredible. It was just that, well, how could you tell if the other person thought it was as amazing as you did?

There were so many things she wanted to tell him. But mostly she just wanted to apologize and explain that the night before had been a mistake. That yes, he had seen her kissing another guy outside the rest room at Casino Night, but no, it wasn't what he thought. It wasn't a *kiss* kiss. It was an AHUL kiss. The guy just happened to have the right first initial.

The problem was, she couldn't tell him. The AHUL was a secret. *I'll tell him it was a dare,* she thought. *Or I'll just tell him I was really drunk or maybe someone slipped me a roofie. Or maybe I'll tell him all three of those things.*

And then she saw him. He came walking out of the library just as she was walking in.

"Zack," she said.

His lips curled up at the corners of his mouth for a moment, almost imperceptibly, and then became tight and tense.

"I have to talk to you," she managed to say.

Zack let out a sarcastic little laugh. "What do you have to talk to me about?" he asked.

"I just want to explain about last night," Jodi said.

Zack's eyes narrowed. "What's there to explain?" he asked. "It's no big deal. It happens all the time—a guy goes to the bathroom, comes out of the bathroom, and there's his girlfriend making out with a guy waiting on line. I'm sure it happens to everybody. I'm glad you did it. Actually, I want to thank you. You took a very ordinary everyday experience for me and turned it into something new and different. I just hope it hasn't scarred me for life. I mean, I hope it hasn't emotionally traumatized me. I hope I'm not going to be one of those guys who just stands at a urinal with his dick hanging out unable to pee because for some reason he can't piss in a public rest room.[5] Or maybe it will be too traumatic for me to even walk into a public rest room. I'll always be afraid of what I'm going to see when I open the men's-room door and walk out again. Maybe I'll just wear Depends."

"Maybe you should wear Pampers, because you're acting like a baby," Jodi shot back. Actually, he sounded like a lunatic. What the hell was he talking about? Men standing at urinals with their dicks hanging out, unable to pee?

"*I'm* a baby?" Zack yelled. "Is that your idea of an apology? Because it's not too effective."

"You're not giving me a chance to explain," Jodi said, looking into his eyes. He was so adorable. She took a deep breath.

"What is wrong with you?" Zack demanded. "If you want to go out with that guy you kissed, then do it. Just leave me alone."

Jodi winced. "I don't want to go out with him," she said quietly, her bottom lip starting to quiver. "I didn't even want to kiss him."

"Okay, so then it was what? Some kind of weird kissing bandit kind of a thing? PU has a kissing bandit on the loose and you were his latest innocent victim?"

Actually, I am *kind of the kissing bandit,* Jodi thought.

Zack waited a moment for her to say something, and

5 Pee freeze—it happens to girls, too.

when she didn't, he just went on ranting at her. "Or maybe the guy was just irresistible, kind of like Fonzie."

"Fonzie?" Jodi echoed blankly. Who was Fonzie, one of the Muppets or something?

"You know, Fonzie. The Fonze. From *Happy Days*. You know, aaaaaayyyy." He stuck both of his thumbs up in the air. "He snaps his fingers, and all the babes instantly start making out with him."

The ache in Jodi's stomach was even worse right now than it had been when Zack had caught her kissing that Lucas guy the night before. Zack was hurt. Really hurt. Why else would he be rambling on about things like *Happy Days*? At least he hadn't just walked away, which he could have so easily done. As long as he was there talking to her, Jodi still had a chance to make him understand somehow.

"I mean, if you don't mind my asking, why exactly *did* you kiss that guy?" Zack asked.

Finally! Jodi's breath caught. "I kissed him because his name was Lucas," she blurted out.

Zack's mouth dropped open in disbelief. "Oh, well, that makes sense," he said. "A guy's name is Lucas, and you just have to kiss him. That's totally understandable. Okay, well, I have to get going now." He started to walk past her.

"Wait!" Jodi said.

Zack turned around.

"I only kissed him because his name started with *L*."

Again Zack turned and just walked away.

"Zack, please," Jodi said. She ran after him and blocked his path. He stopped walking but leveled her with a nasty glare.

Suddenly the truth started pouring out of her. "See, Ali and Celeste have this list. Well, actually it's more of a contest. And I'm doing it with them. I mean, I was. I mean, it's just a game, but I started it before I met you and . . . well, it's kind of a commitment."

"A commitment to what?" Zack said, his eyebrows scrunched together in confusion. But at least the anger was easing out of his features. Jodi took it as a sign she was on the right track.

"It's really no big deal, it's just sort of hard to explain," she went on. "Okay, so this is the thing. We each have to hook up with—well, actually, only kiss—one guy for every letter of the alphabet, in alphabetical order—going by the first letter of their first name. And I was up to *L,* and the guy on line was named Lucas, so I kissed him. But it doesn't mean anything."

Jodi let out a huge sigh of relief. She had explained it. It was all out in the open. She watched Zack's expression, waiting for his familiar cute grin to appear now that he knew the kiss had really been nothing. But strangely, a few seconds passed without so much as a twitch.

"So," he finally began, his voice low, "what you're saying is you and your roommates have made a game out of being skanky sluts." His cheeks grew redder with every word out of his mouth as Jodi felt her own face pale. "That's really great. How very nice for you. I mean, I'm soooo glad we had this talk, because I just thought you had another boyfriend, and now I see that you're actually a whore who kisses guys she doesn't even know or like. Well, it seems you've really adjusted to college life. Have fun." And with that he stormed off.

3

As Celeste had very rightly pointed out, Ali's having the money to pay her tuition—and finally having a real job as the assistant to private investigator extraordinaire Milton Copley—was only half of her problem solved. And the other half seemed pretty much insurmountable. Even though Ali had improved her grades a little bit, she was still very behind—still basically on the verge of failing.

Ali sat at the desk in her room, swinging her legs like a little girl. Celeste had been helpful. She had tried to help Ali study, and Ali knew Celeste was right, she really did have to buckle down. But studying was so boring.

Studying was a solitary activity, and Ali wasn't into those. Like right now, for instance. She stared at the tree outside her open window and noticed how everything was so quiet and still. It was hard to concentrate in all that quiet. Finally, after she had stared at the same branch on the tree for about an hour, a squirrel appeared.

"Hello, little dude," Ali said to the squirrel. The little

dude looked at her for a moment and then ran off down the tree.

Studying was so depressing. And it was Sunday, so she couldn't even go study in the lounge with her soaps on in the background. The only thing on TV on Sundays was Lifetime Television for Women movies that all started with "based on a true story." Victim movies.[6] It was impossible to study with them on because you always got too caught up in the story.

She could read. She had to read five books for her lit class. She could go over to the Blue Sky Café and read there. Actually, that sounded about as exciting as going to the dentist. No, worse, it sounded as exciting as going to the dentist and being stuck for an hour in the waiting room where the only magazines to read were a three-year-old copy of *Highlights* and the spring issue of *Thimble Collectors Club Digest.* Ali giggled. Actually, she'd always thought the thimble magazine was pretty funny. Just the idea that there were really people who were so into thimbles that they actually had a whole club about them. Who the hell cared about *thimbles?* But then again, people really liked to join clubs, and there were a lot of weird clubs in the world. Even right here at Pollard there were about a hundred different ones. . . .

Hey! Suddenly Ali had a thought. Maybe *she* could start her own book club. She wouldn't have to do all this studying by herself, and maybe she could even have some fun with it all. She could be like the white Oprah. The group could read all the books she had to get through for American lit and discuss them. Then she could write papers based on their discussions. Plus it might impress her teachers, and maybe she'd score a little extra credit. Maybe even a little extra *extra* credit, if a guy whose name started with the letter *R* decided to join the group.

Ali put aside her homework and typed up a flyer on her computer. Then she headed out to make copies and post them up everywhere.

This was perfect.

4

Monday morning Celeste got to her intro to psych class early and totally prepared. Dropping out of the AHUL had left her plenty of extra time to study that weekend.

"Is this Psych 101?" a boy standing next to her seat on the aisle asked her.

"Yes," Celeste said, looking at him quizzically. He was actually cute, but he looked a little like Jordan, a guy Celeste had really liked the first week of school. Jordan had turned out to be extremely gay,[7] like most of the guys Celeste had ever tried to date in her life.

This guy seemed more masculine, though. A little rougher around the edges. For instance, he was wearing mismatched socks.

He was definitely not gay. At least, she was almost positive he wasn't.

"It's my first day in the class," cute nongay boy explained,

7 In fact, he has a boyfriend named Arthur Stewart who makes everyone call him Artha.

"so I wanted to make sure to leave time to get here so I wouldn't be late. You know, I'm always worried I won't be able to find the classroom. I have that clichéd recurring dream that I'm running through the halls completely naked and it's finals and I can't find the room where the final is being held and the other students are pointing and laughing at me. . . ."

"Actually, you *are* late," Celeste said, laughing.

"What do you mean?" the guy asked, looking adorably panic-stricken.

"Well, school started the last week of August and it's mid-November. So you're basically about two and a half months late."

The guy laughed.

"Yeah, I see your point. I hope all the girls in this class are as funny as you are. And as cute."

Celeste blushed and looked down.

"No," he said. "What I meant was, it's my first day in *this* class. I transferred into this psych section from another one because I heard this professor is Adlerian, and my last prof was strictly Piaget. And I hate Piaget."

Celeste blushed again. Or maybe it was just a continuation of the original blush. This guy was masculine *and* intellectual. With a bit of the absentminded professor thrown in.[8] Not a bad combination.

"What do you think about Jung?" Celeste asked. "He'd certainly have an interesting interpretation of your dream about being naked and everything."

□□□□□□□□□□□□□□□□□□□□□□□□□□□□□□□□□□□□□

8 The socks.

She immediately wished she hadn't said the word *naked.* "I—I mean," she stuttered, "I've had that dream, too."

"Really," he said. "Maybe next time we could have it together and we could both be running naked down the hallway. Then it wouldn't be so bad."

Before Celeste had a chance to even begin to think of something to say to that, the other students started trickling in and class began.

The guy wrote something in his notebook and angled it at Celeste and nudged her. He obviously wanted her to read what he had written. Celeste looked at his note as nonchalantly as possible. *What's your name?* was written in the corner of the page.

Celeste wrote *Celeste Alexander* in her notebook and angled it toward him.

My name is Darius, he wrote back.

That was a nice name, Darius. But she was up to *E.* She had already kissed a guy named David.

Celeste blinked. What was she thinking? She had officially quit the AHUL. It didn't matter what letter she was up to anymore. She felt a momentary twinge of sadness, remembering that she had quit and Jodi and Ali were going on without her. But wasn't this part of the reason she'd quit? So that she could meet a guy with a letter she'd already kissed and think about something other than the list? Like how cute this guy Darius was?

Nice name, Celeste wrote back.

I hate it. Everyone calls me Elbows. It's my nickname. You can call me either one. Whichever one suits your purposes.

That was a weird thing to write. Whichever one suits your purposes. It was almost like he had read her mind that guys with nicknames were the best kind of guy for the Alphabetical Hookup List because official nicknames were legal according to the amendments.

Well, it was just a weird coincidence. And whichever his name was, Darius or Elbows, it was all the same to her. She had quit. Hadn't she? Yes. Yes, she had.

Nice to meet you, Celeste, Darius wrote.

You too, Celeste wrote back.

Celeste? he wrote.

Celeste giggled.

Yes? she wrote back.

Do you think I could look at your notes to make sure I'm up to speed with the rest of the class?

Sure. Anytime, she wrote back.

It felt kind of good to not have the AHUL looming over her. She was making a friend, and that was all. It felt great not having an ulterior motive. She had been right to quit. Jodi and Ali should try it sometime. *Hooray for me!* Celeste wrote absentmindedly in her notebook. Then she crossed it out about a million times so that Darius Elbows wouldn't see it.

On the way out of class Celeste was kind of hoping Darius Elbows would try to talk to her some more, but someone completely different and unexpected approached her instead—Artha Stewart, the boyfriend of Jordan, whom Celeste had mistakenly thought was interested in her way back at the beginning of the year.

"Girlfriend, I know you might feel a little weird around me," Artha stated, walking alongside Celeste as if she had asked him to or something. "I mean, even if Jojo had no clue, it was pretty obvious you had a huge thing for him. But Jordan has told me what a cool *chica* you are. And besides, you have super fashion sense. I have super fashion sense. And judging by the lustrousness of your locks, you clearly know your hair products." He shifted his Prada backpack higher on his shoulder, flashed her a smile, and announced, "So I think it's time you and I became friends."

Celeste didn't even know how to respond at first, but she decided to take it as a sign. Today, since quitting the AHUL, she'd made *two* new friends. That had to mean she'd done the right thing.

"Well, okay," she told Artha. "If you think so."

"Good." Artha gave her another satisfied smile. "Now tell me, aren't those pants she's wearing *so* wrong?" he asked, nodding at the girl walking in front of them. "And speaking of errors in fashion judgment, our prof has got to learn. . . ."

Celeste continued to walk with Artha and nod at what seemed like appropriate times, but her mind was somewhere else completely . . . somewhere starting with a *D*—or an *E,* depending on how you looked at it.

5

Now, Jodi had never been a depressed-type person. But it seemed like she had received one blow after another ever since arriving on campus. First the Buster breakup. Then her father had cut off her allowance, saying it was time she acted like an adult and supported herself. He'd taken away everything but tuition. She'd even had to sell her car. Then she had her heart set on getting into Kappa Kappa Gamma and, of course, didn't.

She'd thought she had really hit bottom when her bed was set on fire, but that was nothing compared to how she felt now.

This really wasn't like Jodi. She had to figure out a way to get herself out of this funk, like score a six-pack of Prozac or something. Or maybe she should get a new job. That would give her something to do, some necessary distraction, and the extra spending money wouldn't hurt.

She walked over to the student services building and looked at the old bulletin board. *Au pair.* Christ, just what she needed. To be elbow deep in dirty Pampers. She sure wouldn't win the AHUL hanging out with three-year-olds. *Tutor.* Great, she could tutor in the library and have to see Zack all day long. *Lose Weight and Earn $$$ in Research Project.* Only if it involved serious amphetamines.

Who was she kidding? She didn't need a job. What she needed was a car. She needed the freedom to get the hell off this campus for a while and clear her head. But she wasn't going to be able to buy a car anytime soon. Not unless she got another job. A classic catch-22.

Well, at least she could walk off campus. Jodi decided to take the rest of the day for herself. She smiled as she started to stroll across campus, remembering that her mother used to call this kind of day "a soothing day for the soul." "Are you going to take a soothing day?" she would ask Jodi. Jodi headed down a brick path lined on either side by giant weeping willows. She was actually starting to feel a little bit better. It's hard to feel terrible when you're surrounded by so much green.

Then Jodi caught sight of a familiar figure up ahead, in front of the social science building. Buster. And he wasn't alone—he was with some girl. They were huddled close together, talking about something that seemed pretty intense. Since when did Buster get intense about anything verbal?

Jodi felt her chest tighten up. Suddenly she was plunged back into her depression, even deeper than before. And since when did Buster go for goth princesses, anyway? The chick was some Vampirella rip-off with multiple piercings and all. They made an absolutely ridiculous couple—Buster in his Fuck You, You Fucking Fuck T-shirt and Gothvira in her long black velvet cape.

Jodi tore her gaze away, hoping Buster hadn't seen her. She had to get away from here, from them, from everything. Breaking into a run, Jodi tore off in the opposite direction. She finally stopped, panting and sweaty, by the PU gates. She leaned up against a tree to catch her breath, then noticed the flyers all around her—Ali's book club flyers. Jodi squinted at one of the flyers, recognizing her own room's phone number listed at the bottom. Then she took in the whole thing and started to laugh. Ali had drawn a picture of a dog wearing glasses on it for no particular reason and had coincidentally listed all the books from her American Lit required reading list, starting with *Lady Chatterley's Lover.* That was the great thing about Ali. Even when Jodi was at her most depressed, Ali could always make her laugh.

Then another flyer caught her eye, mixed in with all of Ali's. It was for Diamond Cab Co. *Drivers Wanted! Flexible Ours!* Jodi's eyes widened. It was like a sign from God, except for the spelling mistake. This was perfect. She wouldn't have to buy a car. She would be able to drive, earn money, and meet new guys all at the same time. And it was so cool. So much better than au pair or tutor or fucking weight-loss guinea pig. There was something very blue-collar working-class about it, too, just like her father's job at the sardine cannery. She'd get a real education to go along with her college education. She'd learn something about people from the school of hard knocks.

And what would Mr. High-and-Mighty Zack, man of the people, have to say about this? She'd just love to see the look on his face when he found out she had a real job in the real world. Driving a cab was almost like a metaphor for real life. Picking up fares, taking them somewhere, having that brief exchange, and then moving on to the next. Plus you got tips! Mr. Travel in the Real World would be stuck in the library stacks, endlessly reshelving books, while she'd be out in the streets with the people. Ha. He'd probably be so impressed, he'd just have to come crawling back to her.

Jodi couldn't wait to apply at the Diamond Cab Company. She hunted around until she found a phone booth near the campus parking lot, then called the number on the flyer.

"Diamond," a gruff voice said.

"Hello," Jodi said. "I'd like to apply for the cabdriver job."

"What, are you a woman or something?" the person asked.

"Uh, yes, I am," Jodi said.

"Hmmm," the person said.

"Is that a problem?" Jodi asked.

"You got to apply in person, Love Bug," the person said.

"Okay," Jodi said. "Then I need a cab. I'm at the front gates of Pollard University and I have long, curly, sandy blond hair, and I'm wearing a blue hand-knit sweater and jeans."

The person snickered. "That sounds very nice, but this

ain't a blind date, Love Bug, I don't really care what you're wearing. Just tell me where you're going."

"To you," Jodi said. "I'm taking the cab to you. To your office, or garage, or wherever."

The person laughed out loud, sounding uncannily like James Earl Jones in that Schwarzenegger movie.[9] "Yeah? I think that's a first. Taking a taxi to apply to be a taxi driver. Sure, Love Bug. Just give him five minutes."

Jodi hung up and took a deep breath, waiting for the Diamond Cab Co. taxi to come and whisk her off campus, the way Cinderella waited for her pumpkin coach.

9 *Conan the Barbarian,* in which Jones plays the evil priest Thulsa Doom.

6

That night at the triple, Ali and Celeste were hanging out, trying to do their homework and getting ready to go to the lounge and do their absolute favorite thing in the world—watch this show called *Bride to Be*. Everyone in their whole dorm watched the show every single Monday. But where was Jodi? It wasn't like her to miss *Bride to Be*.

The show was pure genius. This gorgeous guy who was like a vice president at some big company got to meet twenty girls and "date" them, and each week he narrowed down the field a little. It was totally disgusting and degrading to women, but it was the most entertaining hour television had ever known. Like when the women who didn't get chosen had nervous breakdowns and things and had to be hauled off by an ambulance.

The phone rang for what seemed like the tenth time in the past few minutes. It was yet another person calling about Ali's book group. Celeste couldn't believe so many students were interested in joining.

"What books did you list?" Celeste asked after Ali had hung up the phone. *"The Joy of Sex? The Sensuous Woman? The Story of O?"*

"No, unfortunately the club has nothing whatsoever to do with sex," Ali replied with a frown. "I don't know why these dudes are calling. I'd love to pick those books, but I had to pick the stupid boring books that are on my reading list, and believe me, there's nothing sexy about them. The first one's about some dude named Lady Chatterley. It was written like a hundred years ago."

"Lady Chatterley's Lover?" Celeste asked.

"Yeah."

"Are you crazy?" Celeste giggled. "*Lady Chatterley's Lover* is all about sex. It's one of the sexiest books ever written. It's very sexy and very graphic."

"Shut up!" Ali said.[10]

"I'm serious."

"You mean it's like hot and shit?" Ali asked.

"That's right," Celeste said. "In fact, I think that's the quote they use on the back of the book: 'This book is hot and shit.'"

"Now I'm psyched," Ali said.

Just then Jodi walked through the door, beaming.

"Where were you?" Celeste asked. "We're missing *Bride to Be.*"

"Oh my God, I forgot," Jodi said. "But it was worth it."

"How come?" Ali and Celeste said at the same time.[11]

☐☐☐☐☐☐☐☐☐☐☐☐☐☐☐☐☐☐☐☐☐☐☐☐☐☐☐☐

10 Not "shut up" be quiet—"shut up" no fucking way!

11 Actually, Celeste said, "Why?"

"Because of this," Jodi said, holding out a plastic identification card.

Ali and Celeste stared at it. Neither of them had any idea what it could be. For instance, if Jodi had lost her student ID and gotten a new one, what was so exciting about that?

"What is it?" Celeste asked.

"Put away the homework, forget about going to watch TV, and break out the tequila," Jodi said.

"We don't have any tequila," Ali said.

"Yes, we do," Jodi said, producing a brown paper bag with a bottle of Cuervo Gold. "It's the good stuff. We're celebrating."

"Celebrating what?" Ali asked, instantly shoving aside her textbook. Ali didn't need to be told twice to put away her homework.

"Congratulate me, girls, I just got my hack license. And in only one day!" Jodi announced.

Ali and Celeste looked at each other, totally baffled.

"You're looking at Diamond Cab's newest driver," Jodi said, as excited as if she were saying that she didn't have to attend classes anymore because PU had just awarded her an honorary doctorate.

"Well, I'll drink to that," Ali said, opening the bottle of Cuervo.

"Um, why are you a cabdriver?" Celeste asked.

"It's a great job," Jodi explained. "I get to drive, which is something I've really missed, and I get tips. It's so awesome. And it's a great way to meet men. I'm going to get a totally kick-ass little chauffeur's outfit. Can't you see it with the hat? It will be so cute."

"Well, that's great!" Ali said. "Maybe I'll do it, too. I certainly wouldn't mind meeting some men. Like a Roy or a Rod or a Rick or a Rimbleton . . ."

"Okay, first of all, Rimbleton isn't even a real name. And second of all, you already have a job," Celeste reminded her. "And when you're not working for Milton, you have to be studying."

The phone rang again and Ali answered, ready to take down the name of her new book-group member. But it wasn't for her. It was for Celeste.

"May I ask who's calling?" Ali asked, making her voice sound British like she was Celeste's maid or something. "Your name is what? That's your name?" She put her hand over the mouthpiece. "Celeste, it's for you—it's someone named Elbows."

Celeste took the phone. "Hello?" she said. "Why aren't you watching *Bride to Be* like everyone else?" She cringed, wishing she hadn't said something that stupid.

"What's *Bride to Be*?" Elbows asked. Celeste wondered if she should answer. But before she could make up her mind, he added, "I was actually calling to see if you're up for meeting me at the library so I can go over those psych notes, like we talked about."

"You mean now?" Celeste asked, holding her undrunk shot of tequila.

"Well, yeah, now would be great, unless you're busy or it's a bad time or something," Elbows said.

"No, it's a good time," Celeste said. "I'll definitely meet you there."

"You're leaving?" Jodi said after Celeste hung up.

"Yeah, I've got to help this guy, Elbows, who's in my psych class."

"Wait a minute, dude, weren't you up to *E* in the AHUL?" Ali asked hopefully. "You're not back in the game, are you?"

"Not in the least," Celeste assured them.

"Well, we should at least go watch the end of *Bride to Be* before you go meet him," Jodi said. "Even though it is the most sexist show I've ever seen, we can't miss the whole episode."

"It really is gross," Ali agreed. "Dating those girls is just a game to that dude. And they're all so serious and into it. And he's making out with all of them and acting like they're the one and the whole time it's just one big fantasy game for him."

"Who would do that?" Jodi said.

Celeste looked at them in disbelief. "Uh, we would do it," she said. "I mean, you guys would."

"What are you talking about?" Ali and Jodi said at the same time.[12]

"What exactly do you think the Alphabetical Hookup List is?"

"It's not degrading to women," Jodi protested.

"No, but it kind of is to men," Celeste countered.

"Well, that's different," Jodi said.

☐☐☐☐☐☐☐☐☐☐☐☐☐☐☐☐☐☐☐☐☐☐☐☐☐☐☐☐

12 Actually, Ali said, "What the fuck?"

"And how is it different?" Celeste asked.

"Because the dudes enjoy it," Ali said.

They all cracked up.

"Dude, have fun at the library, and if you happen to run into a Ricardo, tell him I have something for him, if you know what I mean!" Ali called out as Celeste packed up her notes.

Celeste rolled her eyes and left for the library.

Jodi and Ali shrugged at each other. Oh, well, more tequila for them. Plus they could compare AHUL notes. With Celeste out of the game, neither one of them felt particularly comfortable doing it in front of her.

7

When Celeste arrived at the library, Darius, aka Elbows, was waiting for her out front in a striped J. Crew sweater that was just adorable.

That sweater would look especially nice lying on the floor next to my bed, Celeste thought, totally shocking herself because she had never really thought anything like that before.

"Hi," he said. "You look nice."

Celeste smiled. She hadn't even really paid attention to what she was wearing since it wasn't a date, it was just studying. Or actually, note-lending. "Thanks," she said. "You too."

She gently bit her bottom lip, something she had noticed she had started doing lately when she was nervous.

"Shall we?" he asked.

Celeste nodded, and they walked into the library.

"Where do you like to study?" Celeste asked.

"We might as well go to the fourth floor, where the psychology section is."

"Cool," Celeste said. She followed him to the fourth floor, and they set their stuff up on a corner table. The place was totally empty because it was so late. They didn't even have to whisper, which was strange. Celeste took out her psych notes. "So, do you just want to read them, or copy them, or what?"

"I'm not sure," Darius said, looking them over. "Maybe a combination of both."

"Okay, whatever you want," Celeste said. She was sort of proud of her notes, and she couldn't help feeling a little disappointed when he didn't look up in surprise to compliment her note-taking. Wasn't he awed by her ability to keep everything so neat and organized without missing a word the professor said? But he didn't seem that impressed with the notes.[13]

"Oh, that was the week he introduced us to Freud," Celeste said, pointing to the notebook. "He put these chairs together to make a fake couch, and then he had one of us, this gay guy named Artha Stewart, lie down on the chairs and pretend to be in psychoanalysis."

"Artha Stewart?" Darius said.

Celeste giggled. "His real name is Arthur Stewart, but he makes everyone call him Artha because it rhymes with Martha." She didn't mention that in her first week at Pollard, she had totally fallen for Jordan, the guy who ended up leaving her for Artha.[14]

13 Great note-taking ability is usually not on most boys' top ten lists of turn-ons.

14 Girls falling in love with gay guys in their pasts is also not on their top ten turn-on lists.

"Anyway, he played Freud, and he asked Artha to tell him about his relationship with his mother when he was a child, and Artha did this whole hilarious act where he talked about sleeping in his mother's panties, and then he pretended to cry and announced that he was gay. Everyone in the class was on the floor laughing."

"I wonder how he'll demonstrate the psychologist G. C. Williams," Darius said.

Celeste was stumped. "I don't even know who he is."

"He has very interesting theories about courtship rituals," Darius said.

Celeste felt her face getting hot. Darius knew so much about psychology, and everything he said was so fun and interesting. She hadn't been with a guy like this in a long time. It was probably some kind of karmic reward for letting go of the Alphabetical Hookup List. She was being rewarded with what could possibly be a real relationship. But no. If there was one thing she'd learned in college, it was not to get her hopes up too early.

Darius stopped talking for a little while and flipped slowly through her notes. He laughed.

"What?" she said.

"I like this little thing you do where you turn the holes of the loose-leaf paper into cats."

Celeste cringed. She always drew ears and whiskers around the holes. It was something she'd done ever since she was in elementary school. "Actually, they're foxes," she mumbled.

"Well, I think they're cute. I also like the way you bite your bottom lip like that."

Celeste immediately unbit and looked down.

"So?" Darius said.

"So what?" Celeste asked.

"So? Don't you want to know more about G. C. Williams?"

"Actually, I do," Celeste said. "I've never read anything by him."

"Let's go to the stacks and get some of his work," Darius said.

"Okay, Elbows," Celeste said, trying to make his nickname sound normal.

"Why don't you call me Darius?" he said, smiling. "I mean, everyone else calls me Elbows, but it would be kind of nice if you called me Darius."

Celeste's heart was sort of pounding as they made their way through the rows of shelves. That part of the library was really poorly lit, and it took a while for her eyes to adjust to the darkness. But Darius seemed to know where he was going, and they finally found the psychology books all the way in the back.

"Check it out," Darius murmured in her ear.

Celeste took the book he handed her, opened it, and clapped it shut, causing a big cloud of dust to mushroom up. She let out a nervous giggle. Something about this was making her feel very jumpy. Maybe it was the fact that the library was so deserted. Or maybe it was Darius whispering in her ear like that. Or maybe it was the book itself. In her hands it felt like a books of spells, a sorcerer's tome of tricks.

Celeste opened the book again and flipped through the pages. "Let's go back to our table," she said. "It's too dark. I can't even read the print."

"I can give you the gist of it," Darius said, standing so close behind her, she could feel his hot breath against the back of her neck. "Williams writes about the sea horse. You know what makes the sea horse so fascinating?"

Celeste smiled to herself because she imagined that if Ali were there, she would say, "Uh, nothing." But Celeste instead said, "What?"

"The females go after the males," he said. And then suddenly he was all over her—his body pressed up against her back and his hands reaching around to grab her breasts.

"Now I know why they call you Elbows," Celeste said, trying to lighten up the mood. But he just kept groping her. "Hey," she said lamely. He didn't stop, and he started kissing her neck. "Hey, stop it," she said, her heart starting to race now from fear, not excitement. This was horrible. She felt like a baby, but this wasn't right. What the hell was he doing? "I'm not a sea horse," she said, trying to push him off her. Suddenly she remembered the huge book in her hand and she used every bit of strength she could muster to wriggle out of his grasp and hit him across the face with it.

"Ow, shit," he said, holding his hand up to his face. His

cheek was badly cut. He pulled his fingers away and looked down at them, seeing the blood. "What the hell is wrong with you?" he spat out.

"What the hell are you doing?" she shot back, breathing hard.

"What the hell are *you* doing?" he yelled. "I'm supposed to score. I know you didn't get past *E.* I told you my name's fucking Darius and my nickname is fucking Elbows. *D* or *E,* I had you covered. Elbows starts with an *E,* or maybe you thought it started with an *L.*"

Celeste felt her heart stop. *Oh my God, oh my God.* Her heart had stopped, but her mind was racing. Maybe she had misheard him. There was no way he could know about the AHUL. Jodi and Ali would never have betrayed the secret, not for anything or anyone. "I—I don't know what you're talking about," she stammered.

But Darius or whatever his name was just sneered. "I know all about your little game," he said. "My buddy Picks gave me the 411."

Celeste suddenly felt like she was going to throw up. How could this guy know? And who was Picks?

"I'll tell you how I know if you give me a hand job," he said.

"And I thought chivalry was dead," Celeste said. She threw the book down on the floor, turned, and stomped off. She walked as quickly as possible without running because she was slightly afraid he would follow her, but she didn't want to look afraid.

"Fucking prude!" she heard him yell behind her. "I transferred out of a good psych class for you! Now I'm stuck with a fucking Adlerian! I hate Adler!"

"Well, you should go to the first shrink who will give you an appointment, you fucking wack job!" Celeste yelled back at the top of her lungs. Then she burst into a run.

8

Celeste wasn't going to stop running until she got to her dorm, but then she saw the campus security office on her way. Maybe she should report that asshole and try to get him expelled. Creeps like him shouldn't be allowed on campus. She shuddered, thinking of what could have happened if she hadn't been able to get away from him.

But then she started thinking of all the reasons not to turn him in. For one thing, she wasn't even sure if she knew his real name. And what if he got mad and came after her again? Plus he somehow knew about the AHUL, and what if he started telling a lot of people about that? What if he told the dean? Fuck, what if he started giving a lot of guys their number?

No, she couldn't think about all of that. This guy was scary, and she should report him. Here and now. It was the right thing to do.

Celeste walked up to the CS office entrance and

walked inside. While most of the buildings on campus were big and bright and airy, the CS building seemed like it came straight from the seventies, right down to the bright orange tile designs on the walls and the depressing brown carpet. And it smelled funny, like old tobacco and rotting milk. Celeste walked up to the campus police officer sitting behind his rusty metal desk. He looked like a nice person, kind of short and balding. He had a mustache, and she got the feeling that he was probably someone's uncle. He was just sitting there, tapping his fingers on his desk. He smiled at Celeste. "What can I do for you?" he asked.

Suddenly the last thing she wanted to do was explain to this guy what had happened. She imagined herself telling the story. Well, you see, Mr. Nice Policeman, sir, he was talking about the mating rituals of starfish. No, it was blowfish. No, I'm sorry, it was sea horses. And, well, you see, my friends and I kiss men in alphabetical order, and that's what started this whole thing.

Now that she realized how crazy her story would sound, she just couldn't go through with it. She was too exhausted to even try to explain. "Sorry—I'm in the wrong building," she mumbled, and ran out before he could stop her. And this time she didn't stop running until she was on the second floor of Maize Hall. Apparently some people had been having a fantastic time while she'd been getting attacked in the library: There were plastic Solo cups all over the hallway, the floor was strangely sticky, and from inside one of the rooms someone was screaming (or was that supposed to be singing?), *"Can I take you hoooooome, where we can be aloooooone. . . ."*

As Celeste neared room 213 the horrible sound got louder and louder until—*ugh*—she realized it was coming from *her room.*

Normally Celeste would have found the whole situation sort of funny. Coming home late at night and finding a dorm full of drunk people . . . that was so "college." But after what had just happened, she was so *not* in the mood. She just wanted to get in her bed and tell Jodi and Ali what had happened. And then wash her face and brush her teeth and lie in her bed again and cry for a while. (Actually, just this once she was willing to forgo the face-washing and teeth-brushing part.)

Unfortunately, when she opened the door, she found Ali and Jodi and their next-door neighbors, lazy-eyed, narcoleptic K. J. Martin and Hallie Tosis, doing karaoke on Hallie's karaoke machine, which for some horrible reason was in their room. Hallie was belting out a unique version of "I Love Rock 'n' Roll" and lazy-eyed, narcoleptic K. J. Martin was asleep on Celeste's bed, like some kind of oversized, putrid-smelling Goldilocks. And Jodi had blue stuff all over her face. And wait . . . had Ali stuffed her bra?

The whole room smelled like death—a poisonous gumbo of Hallie's breath and a nearly empty bottle of tequila.

Actually, there wasn't enough tequila left in the bottle for a worm to drown in.

Celeste wasn't the kind of person to make up mean names for people, but after the first couple of experiences with Hallie Thompson's breath, the name Hallie Tosis had really stuck. And lazy-eyed, narcoleptic K. J. Martin? Well, they didn't always call her that. Sometimes they called her LENKJM.

Celeste tried to get Jodi's and Ali's attention, but it was impossible with Hallie practically swallowing the microphone.

"Look at me!" Hallie shouted, breathing into Celeste's face. "I'm Joan Jett meets Britney Spears."

You wish, Celeste thought, cringing. *Try Lassie meets Rosie O'Donnell.* Actually, it should have been Lassie meets someone English, because Hallie was English, but at that moment all Celeste could think of was the Queen Mum, and that didn't seem quite right. Hallie was always saying, "You're a superstah!" to everyone. It was the most annoying thing in the world.

"Hey, Britney, give it a rest," Ali told Hallie. She giggled drunkenly and took a swig of tequila. She handed the bottle to Celeste, who looked at it wearily. All that was left was backwash. It looked like pee. Celeste just shook her head. She felt her throat tightening. Her eyes began to burn. The seriousness of what had happened to her that night—and what had almost happened—was really hitting her now, and she felt like she was about to burst into tears.

"Put another dime in the jukebox, baby," Hallie wailed. "I'm a superstah!"

Hallie waved the microphone in Celeste's face. It smelled foul, just like her breath.

Celeste made a single pathetic sobbing sound into the microphone. She burst into tears—then bolted.

9

Jodi and Ali looked at each other.

"Whoa," Jodi said. "What was that about? She must be really upset about something."

"I know, seriously," Ali said. "I don't think I've ever seen her like that before. Should we go after her?"

Hallie stopped singing into the microphone and turned off the karaoke machine.

"I don't know," Jodi said. "Maybe she wants to be alone."

"Dude, you could be right," Ali said. "We don't want to upset her more."

They had to figure out what was wrong, and it didn't help that lazy-eyed, narcoleptic K. J. Martin chose that moment to wake from the dead. "Is 'Ray of Light' cued up yet? I'm ready to rock," she said, wiping drool from the corner of her mouth. "Or I'll do anything by Jewel."

"Dude, we don't have anything by Jewel, but you could do something by Drool," Ali said.

Lazy-eyed, narcoleptic K. J. Martin ignored her and looked

at Hallie. "You know, when my little sister comes next week, we should have another karaoke night. She's a great singer, too. I guess it runs in my family or something. Sometimes we do 'Gangsta's Paradise' as a duet, and it sounds totally awesome." Her little sister's visit. It was all she had been talking about lately. As if anyone really cared about her stupid little sister. Hallie nodded very seriously while swaying back and forth as though to keep herself from falling over. "You guys can help me show her around," lazy-eyed, narcoleptic K. J. Martin offered. "Oh, but I don't know if I remembered to tell you this one kind of weird thing about her. Unfortunately, she has a condition called narcolepsy. That means she just falls aslee. . . ." With that, she passed out on Celeste's bed again.

Ali ignored her and looked back at Jodi. "So, you really don't think we should chase after Celeste?" she asked.

Jodi met her gaze and considered it for a second, then, without another word, they both jumped up and ran out of the room, even though neither of them had any idea where they were going to find her.

They checked Hallie and LENKJM's room and the dorm den, but she wasn't there. They left Maize Hall and were about to ask someone if they had seen Celeste when Ali spotted her sitting on a bench several yards away. They walked over and tentatively approached her. She was sobbing—crying really, really hard.

"What's wrong?" Jodi asked.

Celeste was silent.

"Celeste, what is it?" Ali asked.

Celeste just shook her head and continued to choke out sobs, trying hard to stop crying.

It was a bench for two, but Jodi and Ali squeezed in on either side of Celeste and each put an arm around her.

A couple of people walked by and stared at them. They probably made an odd picture, crammed onto the bench, but Ali and Jodi were too drunk and too concerned about Celeste to care.

"Why don't you tell us what's wrong?" Jodi asked.

"It's nothing," Celeste said.

"You're crying your eyes out about nothing?" Ali said. "Come on, maybe we can help."

"I'm just being a big baby," Celeste said between sobs.

"Okay, but could you just move your elbow a little to the right?" Ali asked. "It's jabbing me in the ribs."

"Ugh, please don't say the word *Elbow*," Celeste said, crying harder.

"Uh, why can't I say . . . ?" Ali stopped before the word *elbow*.

"Celeste, please tell us what's wrong!" Jodi said, raising her voice. She was starting to get really worried.

And then the whole story started pouring out. The way you give your girlfriends every tiny little detail about a date, that's how Celeste told the story about what Elbows had done to her in the library. She told them everything that had happened—how he had lured her to the darkest, most deserted part of the library and then pushed her up against the books and started groping her.

Ali and Jodi were totally disgusted.

"But that's not the worst part," Celeste said.

"Did he hurt you?" Ali asked.

"No, not really," Celeste said. "I actually hurt him when I smacked him with the book."

"Dude, that rocks," Ali said with a proud grin.

"So, how did it get worse, then?" Jodi asked.

"He knows!" Celeste blurted out. She buried her face in her sleeve like an injured bird and started crying again.

"He knows what?" Ali asked.

Celeste didn't say anything. She just cried quietly.

"Dude, you look pretty when you cry," Ali said. "I always look like my face was run over by a bus when I cry, but you look really *pretty.*"

"Really?" Celeste asked, looking up. It made her feel a little better to think she looked pretty.

"What does that moron know?" Jodi asked.

"He knows about . . ."

Jodi and Ali looked at Celeste in complete frustration. They couldn't imagine anything that they would care about this guy knowing.

"About . . ."

"Celeste, what the fuck does this guy know about?" Jodi demanded. "And who cares what he knows or doesn't know, anyway?"

"He knows about the Alphabetical Hookup List," Celeste finally said. She let out a huge sigh of relief. It felt so much better to have finally told them.

Jodi and Ali were stunned silent, and the three of them sat there quietly, squeezed together onto the bench, until Ali asked the obvious question that had been on all their minds. "How?"

"Yeah, how? How does that fucker know about the AHUL?" Jodi asked. "None of us told anyone, right?"

Celeste and Ali shook their heads solemnly.

"Not even when one of us was incredibly drunk and hanging out till all hours at Dimers?" Jodi asked, looking at Ali.

"I didn't tell anyone, I swear," Ali said.

"Well, if none of us told anyone, then how . . ." Jodi trailed off as she suddenly had a very disturbing thought: *Zack.*

Zack monopolizing her thoughts was nothing new. She'd been having damn near constant Zack thoughts ever since they first made out at the library that one time. Only this was different. She wasn't thinking about how funny he was, or how nice his smile was, or how very cute it was the way his hair was always sticking out all over the place (and sometimes he'd absentmindedly run his fingers through it, which only made it worse), and she wasn't thinking about how horrible it was that she had gone and fucked everything up and now he was never going to speak to her again.

She wasn't thinking of any of those things. Just now what she was thinking was more along the lines of: *Oh, shit. Zack.*

"You guys," Jodi mumbled. "I think I know how Elbows found out about the AHUL."

"Wait. What'd you just say?" Celeste asked.

"I said, I know. I mean, I'm pretty sure I know how Elbows found out. Because see . . . when I was trying to explain to Zack why I was kissing Lucas at Casino Night, I told him about the list."

"You *told* Zack?" Ali said in disbelief.

"Yeah. But I sort of had to because, see, he was really mad about the fact that I was kissing another guy. I tried to explain that it didn't mean anything, but he didn't really seem to understand, so then I told him about the AHUL so he would know that it was really nothing. But then he *still* didn't understand, and I think telling him about the AHUL actually made things worse, because he said that we were being skanky sluts, and so, yeah, maybe it was him. . . ."

"Dude," Ali said, standing up. "Who knew Zack was such an *asshole!* We are *not* skanky. We are *not* sluts. Who does he think he is, saying that about us? I'm going to kick his ass." She stomped one of her platform-boot-clad feet on the grass. "I'm going to kick his fucking ass."

Celeste and Jodi looked at each other and smirked. Even in this incredibly awful situation, the idea of Ali beating up anyone, especially now, when she was dressed in her best Madonna-impression Blonde Ambition mode,[15] was just too funny.

"Whoa, there, cowgirl," Celeste said, grabbing onto Ali's bra strap. "We have to think about this reasonably." She was still upset about what had happened with Elbows, but now, sitting with her two best friends, Celeste felt a lot calmer, and as the only sober one of the three it was good she was

---

15 Bright pink bra over black mesh shirt, bra stuffed with socks to create Madonna-ish cone boobs. Little skirt, giant boots, fake mole painted in appropriate upper-lip area.

there to stop them from doing anything they'd regret later. "Jodi," Celeste said gently, "do you really think Zack would do something that . . . that . . . *crappy?*"

"I guess he must have," Jodi said. "On the one hand, it's hard to believe he'd be such a dick. But on the other hand, no one else knew. He's guilty."

"Wait," Celeste said. "We shouldn't jump to conclusions. Even if Zack was really, *really* mad, I don't know . . . he just doesn't strike me as the rumor-spreading type."

Jodi thought about this for a second. "It's true. He *hates* gossip. He once told me, 'Spreading gossip is worse than spreading herpes. Because at least you can suppress herpes.' That's a direct quote."

"Okay, wait a second. I just thought of something," Celeste said. "So let's say he *did* tell people. And yeah, it's out of character, but what if when he did it, it was because he was temporarily insane or something?"

"Dude. *Totally,*" Ali said. "Seeing Jodi kissing someone else made him go out of his fucking mind with jealousy."

Jodi scratched her head. *If that's what happened, then maybe things are okay after all. He can tell everyone that he just made up the rumor as a joke. And if he only did it because he was jealous, it will mean he isn't actually an asshole, he's just really passionate about me.*[16]

"I've heard stories about stuff like this before," Ali said. "There was this girl who went to my high school a really long

---

16 And maybe a little bit nuts, which is always sort of sexy.

time ago. Like when we were kids. And she was dating this really hot football player and everything was great, but then she found out that the football player actually had a girl-friend. And so the first girl was really mad and wanted him to break up with his girlfriend. But then he wouldn't, and so in a jealous rage she boiled his pet rabbit."[17]

"Wow," Jodi said. "Boiling a rabbit. That's fucked up."

With Jodi and Zack it wasn't really so much like that. For one thing, Jodi didn't have a rabbit (their big teeth freaked her out). And even if she did, Zack would *never* boil it. He really loved animals.

"I guess the only thing to do is for me to go and talk to him." Jodi sighed. "Let's go back to the dorm." She was try-ing to sound very serious, but deep down she was kind of excited. If she confronted Zack with what he'd done, then her kiss with Lucas wouldn't seem so bad anymore. Maybe Zack would decide that they were even. They could work things out, and everything would actually be okay again. . . .

When they got back to the dorm, Jodi looked at her watch. It was a few minutes after midnight. That meant that Zack would just be getting home from his job at the library.

"Okay, guys," Jodi said, grabbing her jacket off her bed. "Wish me luck. I'm going to go talk to him."

"Okay, dude," Ali said, laughing. "But make sure he treats you with some *R-E-S-P-E-C-T.*"

Oops! With all the recent excitement, Jodi had forgotten

17 This did not actually happen in Ali's high school—this is a famous scene from *Fatal Attraction,* a movie starring Michael Douglas and Glenn Close, first released in 1987.

about her own drunk-karaoke costume. Her hair was piled on the very top of her head in a big eighties-style ponytail with little pieces sticking out in every direction. Before Celeste had come in, Jodi had been getting ready to do her version of Aretha Franklin's "Natural Woman." For some reason,[18] she'd let Hallie style her hair. "You'll look like a superstah," she'd promised. And then, for some reason,[19] Jodi had agreed to let lazy-eyed, narcoleptic K. J. Martin do her makeup. But of course lazy-eyed, narcoleptic K. J. Martin had dozed off in the middle, so Jodi had a big blue streak running down the side of her face.

Jodi imagined what Zack would say if he saw her looking like that. He'd probably have some sort of clever joke or comment. That was another thing that was so great about him: He was totally able to appreciate things that were silly and ridiculous. Unlike Buster. Buster's sense of humor had mostly revolved around blonde jokes and fart jokes and jokes about shit and piss. He was also the type of guy who'd watch *America's Funniest Home Videos* because he liked seeing people get hit in the crotch.

Jodi took her towel and her bar of Dove and walked down the hall to the bathroom. As she washed her face she thought some more. She was actually starting to feel pretty happy about the whole thing. Okay, jealousy overall was not a good thing, but if Zack was capable of being that jealous,

□□□□□□□□□□□□□□□□□□□□□□□□□□□□□

18 A reason spelled *T-E-Q-U-I-L-A*.

19 See above.

that must mean he really, really liked her. She imagined how he would apologize when she confronted him.

"I'm so sorry, Jodi," he'd say. "I was just so jealous because I think we're so perfect together. I want to be with you forever." Then maybe he'd give her some sort of present. And then they'd start making out again.

But wait, she was getting ahead of herself. She looked in the mirror. There was still a faint blue stripe down the side of her face, and her hair was a complete mess. But it was getting close to twelve-thirty, and she knew Zack sometimes went out after work. If she didn't hurry over, she might miss him.

10

The walk over to Zack's dorm sobered Jodi up considerably, and she started to get nervous. She hadn't seen Zack at all since they'd had that fight and he'd stormed off. She was suddenly very, *very* thirsty and had a feeling she was getting a terrible case of Hallie Tosis breath.

She opened the heavy glass door and stepped into the giant lobby. To her right was a bulletin board with a bunch of signs tacked to it: PIZZA PARTY IN 4TH-FLOOR LOUNGE,[20] DECORATION COMMITTEE MEETING AT 7:30, and CHRISTINA SFEKAS FOR DORM PRESIDENT. In front of her was the information desk, where a very dorky-looking boy was reading a copy of *Teen Beat* magazine (when she walked in, he tried to hide the cover, but Jodi saw it, anyway). And to her left was a Pepsi machine. Thank God, since it's really hard to concentrate on a serious conversation when your mouth tastes like an old shoe.

□□□□□□□□□□□□□□□□□□□□□□□□□□□□□□

20 The word *pizza* had been crossed out and replaced with *naked.*

Last year Pepsi had given PU something like twenty-five million dollars for the campus to build a new basketball stadium. It was a "gift," but ever since, Coke machines had not been allowed on campus. And there were Pepsi machines *everywhere.*

"Damn Pepsi," Jodi muttered under her breath. It was *so* not her favorite ("Generation Next"—what the hell was *that?*), but she wasn't really in a position to be picky.

She fished all the change out of her pocket: fifty cents. *Shit.*

As if by some kind of magic, a quarter fell from the sky and clinked into her palm.

"You know, drinking that stuff just supports a capitalist society that allows its people to be enslaved by evil corporations," a voice came from over her shoulder.

Capitalist society . . . evil corporations . . . only one person Jodi knew talked like that.

She put her quarters into the machine and pressed the button. Her heart was pounding.

"There's no sugar in this." Jodi leaned over, took her can out of the slot, and popped it open. "It's diet." Okay, so her answer didn't make all that much sense, but it sort of seemed like it did, if you didn't think about it too hard.

Jodi turned around slowly.

And there he was—*Zack.*

Maybe it was suddenly being this close to him, or

maybe it was because she was in that weird place between drunk and hungover, but Jodi was suddenly feeling really light-headed. She leaned against the soda machine. He smirked.

"I was just on my way to meet a friend." He didn't quite look happy to see her, but he didn't look entirely unhappy, either.

"Yeah," Jodi said. *Is he going out to meet another girl? A date that starts at 1:00 A.M. usually means one thing.*[21] "Um, I kind of need to talk to you about something."

"You do?" His face softened slightly. "Hey. What's this all about?" he asked, staring at her hair. "*Cosmo*'s 'hottest new look'?" He made air quotes with his hands.

"Karaoke night," Jodi explained. She could feel her face getting red. "I was doing Aretha."

"You could keep birds up there." He reached out and touched her hair gently. "I can just see the headline: 'The Amazing Jodi Stein Saves Species of Rare Owls from Extinction. . . .'"

He'd called her amazing. And he didn't even sound mad anymore. He must know that she'd found out about the rumors. Maybe he was ready to apologize? Or maybe he was drunk . . . she thought she could smell alcohol on his breath, or maybe that was her own breath she was smelling. . . .

"So what did you want to talk to me about?"

□□□□□□□□□□□□□□□□□□□□□□□□□□□□□

21 Booty call.

"Well. Um." *Damn*, Jodi thought. *Why is this so hard?* She wasn't a shy person by any means. But somehow right now standing with Zack she felt like—God, she felt like she was in seventh fucking grade. "About the other day . . ."

"Yeah," Zack said. "I've been thinking about that, too." He put his hands in his back pockets and rocked on his heels. His pants started to come down just a little bit. He was wearing a piece of blue nylon rope for a belt.

"I wanted to . . . ," Zack said.

"It's just that . . . ," Jodi said at the same time. "You go first," she said, fiddling with the top part of her soda can.

"No, you go," Zack said.

Jodi took a deep breath.

"Well, okay, so. Well, remember that thing I told you about, that stupid Alphabetical Hookup game that I was playing with my roommates? Well, it's like this: Somehow people started finding out. Like, this guy Elbows practically tried to rape Celeste. And he said that he knew all about our game, and I think lots of other people know now. And I pretty much figured out that you had to be the person who told people. I know you only did it because you were jealous or whatever, but I still think it was a pretty fucked-up thing to do. . . ." She trailed off. God, she sounded like such a *dork,* and maybe she was being a little harsher than she meant to be, but at least she'd gotten it out. She'd said what she needed to say.

Zack looked at her and blinked. Once. Twice.

"Wait. What?" He started shaking his head very slowly, like he couldn't understand her. "Is *that* what you came over here for?"

"Well, yeah. This Elbows guy was being a real asshole to Celeste and . . ." Jodi was starting to feel sick to her stomach. Why did Zack look so confused?

"I thought you came over here to apologize. And I was thinking of maybe *forgiving* you. But you actually came over here to *accuse me of spreading rumors about you?* You've got to be kidding! First of all, I don't spread rumors. I already told you that. And second of all, even if I did, do you really think I'd want other people to know that my girlfriend cheated on me because of some game? That what we had meant so little to you that you destroyed it all just to put a fucking letter on some fucking list? Even thinking about it makes me ill."

And with that he walked past her and out the door into the cool night air.

Jodi just stood there, her mouth hanging open. *Oh my God.* Zack really hadn't done it. He hadn't told anyone about the AHUL. She'd just made a serious fool of herself and pushed Zack even farther away. In the past two weeks she'd had only two conversations with Zack—and both had ended with him storming off.

"Shit, shit, shit," Jodi said quietly. Things had already been over, but now they were really, *really* over. She'd messed them up so fantastically, there wasn't even the slightest chance of fixing them now. And not only had she screwed up her chances with Zack, but she was back to square one with figuring out how that freak-boy Elbows knew about the AHUL. Because if Zack was really the only person they'd told, and Zack hadn't spilled the secret . . . then how had it gotten out?

11

While Jodi visited Zack, Ali and Celeste got ready for bed.

"I don't know what the big deal is," Ali fumed as she changed into a T-shirt and boxer shorts. "I mean, this is America, right? We're allowed to kiss anybody we want in any order we want, right?"

Celeste didn't respond, but Ali had plenty left to say, anyway. "I'm not going to let this little jerk ruin our competition. It's ours. I mean, it's hard enough that every single Roopak, Rupert, and Rudyard has suddenly gone into hiding. I'm certainly not going to let this asshole get in the way."

Just then the door opened and Jodi walked inside.

"So did you tell that fucker off?" Ali asked, still too angry to notice that Jodi's face was red and she'd clearly been crying.

"It wasn't Zack," Jodi said miserably, then flung herself facedown onto her bed.

Celeste and Ali exchanged questioning looks. "Are—are you sure?" Celeste asked.

"Yes," Jodi mumbled into her bedspread. She let out a deep sigh, then flopped back over. "He had no idea what I was talking about," she said.

"So then how the fuck did that jerk know about the list?" Ali demanded.

Celeste blinked, remembering something else that Darius/Elbows had said. "Picks," she blurted. "He said something about his friend Picks telling him."

Jodi frowned. "Who the hell is Picks? And could you have maybe thought of that *before* I stomped over to Zack's dorm and screwed up any chance I might still have had with him?"

Celeste winced. "Sorry."

Suddenly the phone rang. Nobody made a move to answer it. They just stared at it as if it were some kind of detonating device.

The answering machine picked up, and whoever it was started to leave a message.

"What's up, ladies?" an obnoxious-sounding guy's voice said. "Please allow me to introduce myself. One of you, the shy one, knows me as David. And one of you, the jocky one, knows me as Lucas. The party girl knows me as Mark. My real name is Will, but that doesn't really matter now. What matters is that if you don't want this little game of yours to be written up in the *Pollard Spectator,* not to mention *The New York Times,* where my uncle happens to work, you're going to be doing me a few favors."

The girls shuddered. Celeste wrapped her bathrobe

tightly around herself, as if he were actually there in the room with them and not just a voice on the answering machine.

"Anyway, ladies, sleep tight. I'll be in touch."

Click.

Celeste went to the door and locked it, which was something they never did.

Then she got back into bed, pulling her comforter around her.

"Shit," Ali murmured. "The guys with that fucking guitar tattoo—they *were* all the same guy."

"Picks," Jodi said, feeling like one of those cartoon lightbulbs had just lit up above her head. "Think about it—it's gotta be the same guy. He probably goes by Picks because he plays the guitar or something."

"Dude, you're right," Ali moaned. "But still, how did he find out about the list? I mean, he's known for a *while*. Way before you told Zack, Jodi, so he definitely didn't do it.[22] The guy made a move on every one of us."

"At least you never kissed him," Celeste said, feeling pretty repulsed by the fact that she had.

"What do you think he meant by that favors thing?" Ali asked.

Celeste and Jodi didn't respond.

"Maybe he's bluffing," Jodi finally said. "He's probably just trying to freak us out since his asshole friend didn't get

□□□□□□□□□□□□□□□□□□□□□□□□□□□□□□□

22 Jodi did not need to be reminded of this right now.

lucky with Celeste tonight. Let's just get some sleep, okay? We all need it. Then tomorrow we'll start trying to figure out how the hell this creep found about the AHUL."

"Yeah, okay," Celeste agreed.

The three girls closed their eyes and hugged their pillows, trying very hard to get Will's voice out of their heads and fall asleep.

12

When Celeste got to Intro to Psych the next day, she couldn't believe that Darius, aka Elbows, had the nerve to show up, but he did. She also couldn't believe he had the nerve to raise his hand when the professor asked a question.

"Yes, Andrew?" the teacher said when he called on him.

So his name wasn't Darius or Elbows. It was Andrew. He had just said his name was Darius and Elbows because he thought she was up to *D* or *E*. But still, how on earth had he found out about the AHUL, and how did he know what letters she and Jodi and Ali were up to? It was really freaking her out.

She had sat on the other side of the room, in the back next to Artha, in an attempt to hide from Darius/Elbows/Andrew. It worked out nicely—Artha was a great distraction. He spent the whole class writing notes to her about his own interesting opinions on *Bride to Be.* Unfortunately, before she had a chance to leave at the end of class, Andrew cornered her and handed her a note.

Celeste unfolded it and looked at it in disbelief.

Now that I know what you and your friends are doing, we're going to be seeing a lot more of each other. In fact, I've already thought of some favors that you three could do for me and Picks. Don't worry. We'll be in touch. P.S. Thanks for last night, by the way—it was pretty hot. P.P.S. Do you think sitting next to that butt pirate is going to make you any safer?

This guy had to be kidding. Celeste slipped the note into her organizer and put it in her bag. Why was this happening to her? She'd finally done the right thing and quit the list, and now she was being punished for something she wasn't even *doing* anymore.

13

That afternoon, despite a pretty sleepless night, Jodi showed up at the Diamond Cab headquarters for her first day on the job.

She entered the garage confidently, but nobody even looked up to notice how confident she was or how cute she looked in the new forty-dollar sunglasses that she had bought just for this job. She had decided to wear them even though it was raining because they really completed her whole cabbie ensemble. The best part of her look was that she was wearing her hair in two little side braids à la Laura Ingalls Wilder in *Little House on the Prairie,* because she figured if she picked up any hot guys in her cab, they would mostly be seeing her from the back, and braids looked really cute from the back.

A couple of old men with giant beer guts and mangy beards sat on a bench against the wall. Ick. Oh, well, what did she expect? Tons of cute guys working here? A little welcome party thrown in her honor? Maybe not that, but a hello or a nod from the dispatcher in the cage would have been nice.

But she wasn't going to let this hamper her enthusiasm. She was so excited about her new job. This cabdriver idea of hers was a real stroke of genius.

Just to be off campus felt amazing. To be away from classes and big Gothic buildings and all that ivy. Also to try to forget for even a little while about how Zack hated her and to stop wondering how that guy Knees or whatever his name was could have found out about the AHUL. *Are our phones tapped or something?* Jodi thought. *Is our room bugged?* It was just so weird.

She shrugged off those thoughts and looked around the garage. It was an ugly cement structure, with two very different framed posters on the walls by way of decoration. One made sense. It was a poster of the jazz musician Charlie Parker. But the other struck Jodi as very odd. It was a poster of a ballerina's pink toe shoes with a long-stemmed red rose. It looked really out of place.

Finally, someone noticed her. One of the old grizzled guys sitting on the bench looked over at her. "You need a cab?" he asked her in a thick southern accent.

"No. I'm a driver," Jodi said.

"You a what?" the guy asked, surprised.

Jodi giggled. "I'm a cabbie," she said, proudly pulling her hack license out of her bag. "I'm one of you," she added.

"You one of me?" the guy said. He grinned, showing brownish teeth. "Why don't you come over here then and sit by me?" He patted the pleather seat next to him, which was patched with duct tape.

"Uh, I'm okay here," Jodi said.

The other guy didn't even look up from his sports page.

Jodi walked up to the dispatcher's cage.

"Driver Jodi Stein here, ready to report for duty," she said. She immediately wished she hadn't said something quite so dorky.

"Mmmm-hmmm," the dispatcher said, looking down at her through the mesh cage.

The dispatcher was a three-hundred-pound African-American woman. Her head was almost completely shaved, and she wore bright blue eye shadow that went all the way up to her eyebrows.

"Hi, Dakota, remember me?" Jodi said.

"I remember you, all right," Dakota said. Even face-to-face, she sounded just like James Earl Jones. "I'm just a little surprised you showed up."

"Why?" Jodi asked. "I told you I was really excited to begin working."

"I thought you was just one of those annoying kids who's always trying to make a, what do they call it, a student film or something. I didn't know you was serious."

"Well, I am serious," Jodi said.

"You're not a lesbian, are you, Love Bug?" Dakota asked.

"No!" Jodi said, totally taken aback. Maybe the braids, sunglasses, and little jacket had the opposite effect of what she was going for.

"Oh, cuz I am, and Love Bug, you cute," Dakota said.

"Oh, uh, thank you," Jodi said, feeling a little confused. What was this, a women's prison or a cab company?

"What'd you just say?"

Jodi glanced over in the direction of the voice and saw another woman, almost as large as Dakota, walking into the room from a side door.

"Hi, Love Bug," Dakota said. "I want you to meet our new little driver. Her name is Jodi. Jodi, this is Pia."

Pia bore a striking resemblance to a linebacker for the New York Jets. She looked Jodi up and down and made a sucking sound between her two front teeth, then walked back out of the room.

"Oh, don't mind her, Love Bug. She's the jealous type," Dakota said.

Jodi laughed nervously. She didn't know what to say. If she said Pia had nothing to worry about, Dakota might get insulted. Jodi decided just to focus on the job.

"So, when do I start working?"

"You already did," Dakota said. "Half the time, Love Bug, you just sit around here at the garage staring at all of our pretty faces while your ass flattens out like a coupla apple pancakes. That ain't so bad, is it?"

Jodi's ass flattening out like apple pancakes was not a very appealing image. She made a mental note to bring some free weights next time so she could fit in a quick workout while she was waiting for fares.

"Okay, well, I'll be waiting right over there," Jodi said,

pointing at the bench where the other drivers were sitting.

"Good idea, Love Bug," Dakota said.

But before Jodi had a chance to sit down, Dakota called her back to the cage. "Okay, Love Bug, we got one for you. It's an airport run. You're picking up a Peter Smith at the American Airlines international terminal. It's about two hours round-trip. But the tips are always good. Cab 1901. The keys are in the ignition."

Jodi was thrilled—until she saw cab 1901. It looked like 1901 was the year it was built. The white paint was chipped, with black and rust showing underneath it, and the interior was filthy. As she pulled out of the driveway she realized the car had no shocks, and it sounded like it needed a new muffler. And by the time she had gotten about a mile away, she realized good old 1901 needed one more thing: gas. The tank was as empty as her bank account.

"All right, Junkyard Doggie, you're just going to have to make it," Jodi said out loud to the car. Other cars sped by her and honked because she was going too slow. The cute outfit was definitely overkill in this thing. She'd be lucky if she even made it to the airport alive.

After twenty minutes of chugging along, Dakota came through on the radio. "Love Bug, come in, Love Bug."

"This is Love Bug, I mean, Jodi," Jodi said, but Dakota obviously couldn't hear her. Dakota tried coming through a few more times and then stopped.

Well, Jodi had no choice. She had to stop for gas if she was to have any hope of making it to the airport. She pulled into the Exxon station and paid for half a tank of gas with her own not-yet-hard-earned money. Then she stopped at Baskin-Robbins and got herself a coffee milk shake because of the horrible tequila hangover that was making her feel like fingers were poking at her eyes. So, maybe driving a cab wasn't as romantic as she'd expected it to be.

When she finally got to the airport, it wasn't hard to spot her fare. He was the only one left standing sadly on the pickup island, looking at his watch, wearing some sort of khaki safari outfit complete with fanny pack and Panama hat and holding his luggage. And let's just say it wasn't exactly Louis Vuitton.

She pulled up next to him and he got in, leaving his luggage on the curb.

"You forgot your luggage," Jodi told him.

"Oh, yeah, thanks, that would be great, but please be very careful with the big one—there are some fine fossil specimens in that one."

Jodi sat in the driver's seat, baffled for a moment until she realized that he expected her to get his luggage.

"I guess chivalry *is* dead," Jodi said under her breath, using one of Celeste's lines that always made her laugh.

She got out of the cab and struggled to put the luggage in the trunk, but when the trunk wouldn't open, she shoved the bags into the front passenger seat, got back in, and started her first job as a driver.

"Where to?" she said brightly.

"Pollard University," the guy said.

Great. She was just destined never to get off campus.

"Why are you going to PU?" Jodi asked, trying to be friendly. She was pretty sure that was the way to get great tips.

"I'm an archaeology professor there," he said. "I'm returning from a very interesting dig in Mexico."

"Really," she said. "I'm a student there."

"In Mexico?"

"No, at PU."

"I'm sorry, sir, I really can't chat right now. I have some more observations to record in my journal," the professor said, jotting something down in a small book that looked like a little girl's diary.

Sir! He hadn't even noticed that she was a girl. What a dork. Well, not talking was fine with her. She was content to stare at the broken yellow line and have a little time to think, although it was hard to hear her own thoughts above the rattling engine.

She was pretty deep into a full-blown fantasy about Zack hitchhiking on the side of the road, when she would pull up in her trusty cab and pick him up and listen to him tell her how impressed he was that she was a driver, out in the world, out with the people, when suddenly Dakota's voice came in very loudly over the radio.

"Oh, Love Bug, Love Bug," she moaned.[23]

Jodi almost crashed the cab, it took her so much by surprise.

□□□□□□□□□□□□□□□□□□□□□□□□□□□□□□□

23 Dakota's voice coming over the radio was *not* part of the above fantasy.

"Oh, yes, oh, yes, oh, Love, oh, Bug, oh ohhhhhh ohhhhhhhh."

Someone else was grunting in the background.

"Give it to Pia, come on, baby, give it *aaaallll* to Pia."

"Oh, yeah, Love Bug, I'm going to give it to you," Dakota said.

Eeew! They were doing it! Dakota's big ass must have switched on the PA.

"Would you mind turning that off?" the professor said. "I don't know how you kids can listen to this crap on the radio."

"Oh, Pia, baby, it's gonna be big!" Dakota said.

Jodi tried desperately to turn off the sound, but she couldn't.

"Yeah, baby," Pia said. "Make it a big one!"

"Oh, it's gonna be a big one!" Dakota assured her. "It's really gonna be. . . ."

"Yeah, baby, give it to mama."

"It's gonna be . . ."

"That's it, baby. . . ."

"It's gonna be . . ."

And just as Dakota screamed, "Big," at the top of her lungs, the cab's engine cut out and the car began chugging to a stop right in the middle of the highway.

Jodi had no idea what to do.

"That was some damn nice afternoon delight," Pia said over the radio. "Maybe we should do it again."

"Right now, Love Bug?" Dakota giggled.[24]

☐☐☐☐☐☐☐☐☐☐☐☐☐☐☐☐☐☐☐☐☐☐☐☐☐☐☐☐

24 Imagine James Earl Jones giggling.

"Some of the drivers might be coming back soon."

"Oh, come on, we're all alone right now. We have time."

Jodi managed to get the cab over to the shoulder of the road, and the professor called for a tow truck on his cell phone since Jodi couldn't get the radio to work right. She also still couldn't get the volume down, so the two of them sat there for two hours waiting for help,[25] listening to Pia and Dakota making hot lesbian love.

And after all that, to be tipped in pesos?

There had to be a better way.

25 Have you ever called AAA?

14

Well, this was a first. Ali had missed her soaps. She hadn't answered the phone. She hadn't even gone to the dining hall for lunch. That was how engrossed she was in her new favorite book, *Lady Chatterley's Lover*. Boy—it really was racy!

She got out of bed finally to pee and realized that her whole body had stiffened up. Okay, maybe she should take a walk or something. Who knew, maybe her own Oliver Mellors[26] was waiting for her right outside. Only his name would have to start with an *R*. Which would mean his name would be Roliver, which was a pretty ridiculous name. But then again, if he was anything like Oliver from the book, kissing him would be fucking awesome. *Roliver. Roliver Mellors, where are you?* Ali pulled on some clothes and walked across campus, still reading, all the way to the Blue Sky Café.

She was about to enter the café for a coffee when she literally bumped right into Jodi.

26 Oliver Mellors—the "lover" in *Lady Chatterley's Lover*.

"Dude, I hope you drive better than you walk," Ali said.

"Dude, you're the one who's walking and reading at the same time," Jodi said.

"Coffee milk shake?" Ali asked.

"Actually, it's a two-coffee milk shake day."

"Ow," Ali said. She looked at Jodi and laughed. "You really do look like a grease monkey." Jodi's braids were messy, and there was a smudge of dirt across her cheek. "But I mean that in the best sense of the word. How was your first day?"

"I learned something very valuable at the bank today," Jodi said. "Mexican currency is not worth very much when you exchange it for dollars."

"Well, I learned something, too," Ali said. "I went to see Milton Copley today 'cause I was scheduled to work, but he wasn't in his office. Then the guy in the office down the hall told me that Milton fell off the roof in the middle of a stake-out and won't be returning to work for a while."

"Oh God," Jodi said. "That's awful."

"Actually, the guy made it sound like it wasn't too bad. No permanent damage or anything. And Milton was always talking about how one of these days he was going to take a rest. Plus I bet he's getting some really good drugs. But it just sucks for me because now I'm out of a job." Ali frowned. "On the upside, *Lady Chatterley's Lover* has gotten me totally hooked on phonics. Which is convenient, because it looks like I'm going to have a lot of extra time for reading these days."

Jodi laughed. "Hey, here's a job you can do," she said, pointing to a flyer on the café's bulletin board. The flyer said, *Funky, affordable band we need for small, different wedding at PU Chapel. We have only pay $500. Please call Ileana.* Then it gave a cell phone number. "Five hundred bucks? Not bad for one night's work. And considering whoever posted this can barely speak English, it should be an easy sell."

"But I'm not in a band and I don't play an instrument," Ali said.

"So? Dude, I'm surprised at you. You can sing, can't you?"

"Uh, not really," Ali said.

"Oh, come on, you're great at karaoke. Well, you've got a great look," Jodi amended. "And that's the most important quality in the frontperson of a band."

"Well, that's kind of true," Ali said hesitantly. "Maybe the three of us should do it—you, me, and Celeste."

"I played trumpet in high school," Jodi said.[27]

"We need a name," Ali said.

"How about the AHULs?" Jodi suggested.

"Too risky. Everyone will want to know what it stands for."

"Okay, well, how about something with your favorite word, *dude*. Band Dudes. The Georgia Dudes. Or maybe just Dudes."

"That sounds ridiculous," Ali said. "We need something cool. How about The Lady Chatterleys?"

"I like that," Jodi said. She ripped down the flyer, studied it one more time, and handed it to Ali. "Hey, there's

---

27 A fact that had elicited an endless supply of "I've got your trumpet right here, baby" jokes from Buster.

Celeste," she said, looking through the glass doors of the café. "Let's go tell her about the band!"

They pushed open the door and rushed over to her table. "Celeste, you're not even going to believe the idea we just—"

Jodi cut herself off when she caught a glimpse of Celeste's miserable expression. "Celeste? What happened?" She and Ali sank into chairs on either side of Celeste, crowding around her.

Celeste grimaced. "Today after psych class Andrew— that's Darius's real name—gave me this." She pulled out the note and handed it to Jodi.

Jodi read as Ali scanned over her shoulder. "He's just trying to freak you out," Ali declared, sitting back in her chair.

"Yeah, I agree," Jodi said. "Man, what a loser."

"You guys," Celeste said, "I know you think I'm being silly. And I don't want to be making a big deal out of nothing, but I'm really worried about this Picks and Elbows thing. I mean, you didn't see Andrew's face when I looked back at him. He looked so smug and evil. I don't know what they're capable of. They could totally take over our lives. And there'd be nothing we could do."

"Look," Jodi said. "I know you're upset, but I really don't think you need to worry that much."

"Seriously, dude," Ali said. "Except for that one phone call, they haven't said anything else to either me or Jodi. They're probably just picking on you because they think you'll be easy to upset. Elbows knows how much the library thing freaked you out, so he thinks he has all this power over you. But he doesn't."

"Yeah," Jodi said. "I mean, blackmail? Come on, that is so *Saved by the Bell*."

"Yeah," Ali said. "And not even the cool old *Saved by the Bell*. I'm talking *Saved by the Bell: The New Class*."

Celeste smiled. "I have no idea what either of you is talking about."

"Hey!" Jodi said. "I almost forgot! We have something that might take your mind off this whole note thing!"

"What?"

"Well," Ali said. "We're going to start a band. Surprise!"

"You and Jodi?" Celeste asked. "That's great. I can, like, be your groupie. I'll go to every show you guys have and—"

"No, dude. Not me and Jodi." Ali smiled. *"Us.* Like, all three of us."

Uh-oh . . .

15

Jodi had come to an important realization. Her career as a cabbie, albeit short-lived, had to come to an end. She had to quit. Nothing—not even all the tea in China or all the pesos in Tijuana—was worth driving that wreck on wheels around. Dakota would have to find another sucker. Eeew! No pun intended.

Besides, what Jodi really wanted to do was lie in bed and think about Zack. Or sit in class and think about Zack. Or run laps and think about Zack. She really missed him. She talked to him in her mind, explaining what had happened over and over. Sometimes in her mind she would get mad at him and tell him she had every right to do the AHUL and he was just being a big jerk about it, and sometimes she begged his forgiveness and said how sorry she was for accusing him of spilling their secret when he hadn't. But the fantasy always ended abruptly with him walking away, telling her it was over, not understanding or forgiving her at all.

Also, there was something really annoying about having to take a bus to your job as a cabdriver. There was absolutely nothing glamorous, exotic, or exciting about taking the bus. And that was why this was the last time she was going to take it.

She wanted to quit in person and get her paycheck.

Jodi entered the garage to find it the exact same way she had left it. The tired-looking old men were on the bench under the poster of the toe shoe and Dakota was up in the cage. Today it was green eye shadow, though. Maybe to match her green sweat suit? Thankfully Pia wasn't there. Unless she was in the cage but out of sight. Eeew.

Jodi bravely marched up to Dakota.

"I'm afraid I'm not going to be able to work here anymore," Jodi said.

Dakota looked down at her.

"Well, I'm very sorry to hear that, Love Bug," she said. "Genu-wine-ly sorry."

"It just doesn't seem to be working out for me," Jodi said.

"I see," Dakota said. "But that really is a shame." She shook her head sorrowfully.

"Yeah, well, can I have my paycheck now? I mean, I know I only worked one shift, but I'll still get paid, right?"

"I just wish you was working one more little shift."

"Well, I really can't."

"It's funny, 'cause I was just thinking about you."

"You were?" Jodi asked.

"Yes, ma'am. I was noticing you was looking a little glum, Love Bug, and I was thinking that I know just what you need."

"What?" Jodi asked, sort of touched that Dakota had been thinking about her and cared about how she was feeling. Dakota was a little strange, but she was actually quite a nice person.

"What you need is a maaaannnn," Dakota said.

"Huh?"

"You need a man, a nice, good man. If you'll forgive me for saying it, I can tell you're a little, well, *frus*trated, if you know what I'm saying."

"No, I'm not . . . ," Jodi started to say, but then she stopped herself because, well, Dakota was sort of right.

"It's okay, Love Bug, we all get a little sexually frustrated from time to time, and I could tell just by looking at you. At first I thought it was just that your braids was pulled too tight, but then I realized that no, there was a girl who definitely needed some afternoon delight, morning, noon, and night."

Jodi didn't know what to say. "Well, I'll look into that. I mean, I just had a breakup, so maybe I am a little frustrated."

"I have just the guy for you. I mean, I had the guy for you. I mean, it's a real shame you quit just when I was going to give you this fare. His name is Lance, and he's one of our regulars. Every dang Wednesday he takes his sweet old grandmother to the nursing home for physical therapy."

"What a mensch," Jodi said.

"A what?" Dakota asked.

"Nothing," Jodi said. "He sounds like a nice guy."

"Oh, he is. He sure is, Love Bug. And he's cute as a button. It's just too bad you quit is all. Because here it is Wednesday and you'd be the one doing the driving."

Jodi took a moment to think about it. This guy Lance did sound kind of nice. And she *had* taken the bus all the way there, so it seemed a shame to just go home empty-handed. It would make the whole thing worthwhile if she had some money to show for it. Plus she did have the AHUL to worry about. How was she going to win the AHUL if she didn't even try? How was she going to win if total strangers could tell she was sexually frustrated?

"I'll do it," Jodi said. "But this is my last fare. Okay?"

"Whatever you say, Love Bug," Dakota said, handing her the keys to cab 1901.

Jodi groaned. At least it wasn't an airport run. Oh, well, it was all in the name of love.

"Is there gas in it at least?" Jodi asked.

"She's fully loaded," Dakota assured her.

Pia walked into the garage and glared at Jodi, so Jodi hopped in the hellmobile and hightailed it out of there.

When she got to Lance's grandmother's house, they were both waiting outside for her on the porch. Jodi pulled into the driveway and honked. The honk was much louder than she'd expected, and for a second she worried that she might have given the old lady a heart attack.

Lance was really cute. He had curly brown hair, and actually, he looked a little like Zack. No, she wasn't going to let herself think about Zack. *Two points,* she thought. Before she left for college, she had done Weight Watchers for the whole summer so that she'd be coming to campus in top shape, and at Weight Watchers everything you ate counted as a certain number of points. It was like a budget—like you had a certain amount of money to spend in the day, you had a certain amount of points to spend on food in a day. So Jodi was trying to apply the point system to thinking about Zack. She called it Zack Watchers, and she was only allowing herself a certain number of thoughts about Zack each day. A fleeting thought was one point. A more prolonged thought was two points. And a full-blown fantasy was twelve points. She had a limit of twenty Zack points a day, and today she was already up to forty-six.

But back to Lance. Dakota was right. He was cute. And so was his grandmother. She looked like Sophia from *The Golden Girls,* and she had on a totally matching outfit: Lavender blouse, lavender skirt, lavender shoes, and a lavender basket purse with knitting needles and wool sticking out of it.

With Lance's grandmother holding on to his arm, they slowly made their way to the car. Jodi got out of the cab to help. She opened the back door and then waited about an hour for them to make it all the way there.

"Thank you kindly, miss," Lance said, in an absolutely adorable southern accent.

"You can call me Jodi," Jodi said. It was too bad she had already done *L* on the list. But then she remembered that *L* didn't really count because the guy's name hadn't really been Lucas, it was Will. She was *still* on *L!*

"Well, Jodi, you can call me Lance. And this lovely woman—" Lance put his hand on his grandmother's back "—this is my grandma Ettie. You can call her Grandma Ettie."

"Really?" Jodi asked.

"Of course, dear," Grandma Ettie said, smiling. "All Lancey's friends call me that."

"Oh, that's very nice of you, but I'm just the . . . ," Jodi started. She glanced over at Lance and he nodded, smiling. "Oh, okay. Grandma Ettie," Jodi said.

Lance helped Grandma Ettie into the cab.

"So, Jodi, dear," Grandma Ettie said from the back. "Cabdriver, that is certainly an interesting job for a young lady. Are you a student over at Pollard?"

"Yes, I am," Jodi said.

"Well, isn't that nice. You know, my Lancey went to Pollard. Graduated two years ago. Very smart boy, dean's list all four years. Isn't that right, Lancey?"

"Aw, Grandma," Lance said. Jodi glanced in the rearview mirror; he was blushing.

"I have a right to be proud of you, Lance," Grandma Ettie said. "Why, I practically raised you up myself. And I think I did a fine job. Or a 'rocking job,' as you would say, Lancey." She turned to Jodi, "And don't you think he's handsome? And very personable?"

"Yes, Grandma Ettie." Jodi giggled. "Your grandson seems very nice."

"Oh, he *is* nice. And he is a fine upstanding young man, too. A fine upstanding nice young man who loves his grandma."

"Grandma Ettie, stop. You're embarrassing me. So, Jodi," Lance said loudly, changing the subject. "How long have you been driving this wreck?"

"Actually, this is only my second trip," Jodi admitted. They were stopped at a stoplight, so she looked into the rearview mirror again and Lance was staring right at her. Their eyes locked.

"So, you're practically a virgin," Lance said.

"Lance! I never!" Grandma Ettie said. "Back when I was a girl, a gentleman would never discuss amorous matters in front of a lady until he'd known her for at least six dates."

Jodi and Lance laughed. *This is totally bizarre,* Jodi thought. *This is the type of story that Zack would appreciate . . . except for the flirting part of course and . . . ARGH! Three points!*

A *beeeeeeeeep* sound came from behind them.

"Um, Jodi, I'm no driving expert, but I think a green light might mean go," Lance said.

Oops. Jodi blushed.

They were quiet for the rest of the ride to the nursing home, but the whole time Jodi kept looking into the rearview mirror to see if Lance was looking at her. And each time he was. Between obsessing about Zack and flirting with Lance,

Jodi was so distracted that she was amazed they made it to the nursing home without a tow truck. Not that she was in any kind of rush to be in one of those again anytime soon.

"Well, Jodi, dear," Grandma Ettie said once Jodi had stopped the cab. "My friend Gertrude has physical therapy at the same time as I do, so we always get a ride back from her grandson, but it's been lovely meeting you."

"You too, Grandma Ettie," Jodi said. "And, uh, you too, Lance."

"Bye, Jodi." Lance started to lead his grandma inside but stopped right in front of the door. He glanced over at Jodi in the driver's seat of the cab, then leaned down to his grandmother to tell her something. Then, when Grandma Ettie had steadied herself on her little lavender shoes, he asked her to wait a moment and jogged back over to Jodi. She rolled the window all the way down.

"I'll be back to pay you in just a sec," he said. "Let me just bring my grandma inside first. You know, so she won't be late. Do you mind?"

"Not at all, it's my pleasure to serve you." She did a little salute, which she then regretted because she wasn't a soldier, she was a cabdriver. But Lance just winked. Jodi watched him walk inside and tried to get excited by the idea that he clearly wanted an alone moment with her.

What was *wrong* with her? Here was a really adorable guy. A really adorable nice guy who was flirting with her ferociously and really seemed to like her. So why wasn't she thrilled? A few minutes later Lance came back to the cab.

He opened the passenger-side door. "Hey, there, Miss Jodi. Mind if I hang out here in the cab with you? I love my grandma, and the other people at the home are all right. But it smells like rotting cheese in there. And when I come in, someone always gets started about 'kids today' and 'that darn rap music' and then they start saying 'tarnation' and calling me 'sonny boy,' and it turns into a big ol' mess."

"I think it'd be okay if you stayed here with me," Jodi said, giggling. "You know, because you're such a fine upstanding young man and all."

"Oh, yeah." Lance laughed. "I love my grandmother, but she does go on sometimes. I'm twenty-three, but she still stocks her refrigerator full of Hi-C for me when I come over."

"I know what you mean. I think it's always like that with relatives. One year my nana called me up to ask me what she should bring over for my birthday, a Barbie cake or one with a princess on it. That was the year I was turning seventeen."

Lance grinned. "Last year I moved into a new apartment, and Grandma Ettie's housewarming gift consisted of a Harry Potter poster and a new set of bedsheets covered in pictures of race cars."

"Oh, that's so cute," Jodi said.

"Thanks." Lance leaned over close to her. "I think you're cute, too. You're definitely the best-looking cabdriver I've ever gotten from Diamond Cab."

"Well, thank you very much." She beamed. He was so close, his lips were practically within reach.

"I don't think I've ever had a lady cabdriver before. I mean, unless you count Pia," Lance said.

"Well," Jodi said bravely, "I've never had a gorgeous hunk for a passenger before."

Lance blushed. "That's not exactly saying much," he said. "Since I'm only your second one."

"Hmmm, I guess that's a point," Jodi said.

"So, I guess it's pretty safe to say you've probably never kissed one of your passengers before," Lance said.

"Let me think," Jodi said, pretending to rack her brain. "No, I don't think I have. You don't want me to kiss Grandma Ettie, do you? I mean, she seems really sweet and all . . . but she's not quite my type."

"No, ma'am, that's not exactly what I had in mind," Lance said. And then he leaned very close to Jodi and kissed her. *Mmmm, like tasting a ripe Georgia peach.*

And yet . . .

It should have been thrilling. Normally a kiss like that would have been exciting. At the very least, fun. But even though Lance had mastered the art of gentle yet stimulating tongue darts and lip movement—while maintaining a perfect balance of moisture—something was missing.

Jodi closed her eyes, trying to sink deeper into the moment and enjoy the kiss. Hmmm, maybe this wasn't so bad after all. It was getting nicer by the second. She reached up to run her hand through Zack's hair, then—

Immediately Jodi's eyes popped open and she pulled back from the kiss.

This was Lance. *Lance,* not Zack. That's why the kiss wasn't working. Because if there was one thing the Alphabetical Hookup List had taught her, it was that when you need a *Z,* an *L* just won't do.

16

Shoot. Shoot. Shoot. Shoot. Shoot.

Celeste ran through the door of the psych building and down the big granite steps.

Shoot just wasn't cutting it here.

FUCK! She ran across the quad, hands in fists, jaw clenched.

"Celeste?" Artha Stewart called behind her. "Are you okay? What's wrong? Was it that thing I said about Jim Carey's teeth? I don't *really* think they make him look like a horse. . . . I was *kidding.* He's a really great actor. I had no idea you even liked him so much!"

I'll explain everything to him tomorrow, Celeste thought as she continued running, not looking back.

Celeste didn't want to talk to Artha just then or anyone else for that matter. She just wanted to . . . wanted to . . . kick something! Celeste ran up to a tree and got ready to give it a good kick. Then—in light of the fact that kicking the tree might scratch the pair of suede boots she'd borrowed from

Jodi that morning—Celeste decided that a more reasonable thing to do would be to lean against the tree and cry. And so she did.

Anyone looking at Celeste sobbing against the giant oak would probably have assumed she was really sad about something. But actually, she wasn't sad at all—she was mad. Extremely fucking fucking fucking fucking mad. Maybe the angriest she'd ever been in her entire life. After all, Celeste had been brought up by parents who strictly adhered to the rules of the Creative Anger Management Movement. The Creative Anger Management Movement was something that Jib and Carla had taken seminars in while Carla was pregnant with Celeste and they were living on an organic potato farm in Boulder. During these seminars, Carla and Jib had learned that the best thing to do with anger was to use it as fuel for a "creative act," oftentimes through a poem, song, or interpretive dance.

And while Celeste had never gone so far as to make a Fury Mug (as Jib sometimes did), she had little experience in seeing people act really mad and didn't know how to deal with it. And that was why she was crying instead of yelling, even though, considering the situation, it would have been totally understandable had she been screaming her head off.

God, and to think that in the beginning, I actually liked him. The most monstrous, horrible person on earth! I can't believe he's doing this!

Celeste continued running across campus toward Maize Hall. Twenty feet in front of her a boy and a girl were walking with their arms around each other, stopping every so often to kiss.

Sure, you think he seems nice now. But Darius/Elbows/Andrew seemed nice at first, too. Just you wait. . . .

Why did Celeste have such horrible luck with guys? First Jordan had turned out to be gay (which ended up being all right because now she was friends with him and Artha). Then she'd lost her virginity during a stupid drunken one-night stand with that asshole, Buster. After that Carter Mann had turned out to be a creepy pothead loser. But the whole Elbows/Darius/Andrew debacle was by far the worst. . . .

And before that stupid jerk ruined it, I was actually having a really nice day! The weather was perfect, the birds were chirping happily, and Celeste was having a truly excellent hair day. And when she got to class, Artha had sat next to her and revealed that he had the newest issue of *People* magazine hidden inside his textbook.

Celeste usually paid attention in class, but it was just so cute the way he was *so* excited about his magazine. When he invited her to play the Joan and Melissa Rivers game,[28] she couldn't resist.

So they'd spent the first half of class giggling and passing the *People* back and forth, writing funny comments with Artha's bright purple jelly ball.

28 The Joan and Melissa Rivers game was invented by Artha. Players flip through a magazine and make Joan-esque comments about all the models and celebrities. This also makes an excellent drinking game.

Artha had written, *Hello. Try going back to the poodle farm, girlfriend,* next to a picture of Christina Aguilera with her hair brushed out *Moulin Rouge*-style.

And then Celeste had drawn a think balloon over a picture of Lil' Kim (in a multicolored feather outfit) and written, *I hope no one finds out that I am part peacock.*

And then Artha had drawn a talk bubble over Catherine Zeta-Jones and written, *Sure, Michael Douglas might look somewhat birdlike, but I find that very sexy in a man!*

And Celeste had started giggling (although to be honest, she had no idea who most of these people were). And she was thinking, *Wow, this is the first time I've been in psych class without a stomachache since that whole stupid library thing happened.*

And then all of a sudden a folded-up piece of notebook paper had flown through the air and landed smack in the middle of her desk. She'd turned around to see where the note had come from and there was Andrew, sitting a few rows back, looking straight at her. He was waggling his stupid fucking eyebrows and grinning evilly.

This cannot be good, she'd thought. With shaking hands, Celeste had unfolded the note:

> *Hey Sweetheart,*
>   *Glad to see you're having such a nice time with your new friend the pillow biter. I just wanted to let*

you know that I overheard you talking about your paper topic: "The Marquis de SSADY: Sadomasochism, Seasonal Affective Disorder, and You.

I'm totally fucking impressed. Really. It's quite brilliant. So, what I was thinking was that I'd actually like to turn that paper in myself. I figured you wouldn't mind since you're such a smart girl (I'm sure you'll have time to write a new one—after all, you have an entire day, and it only has to be twenty pages). Just bring it in to class tomorrow with my name on the top. I'd really appreciate it.

Your friend,

Andrew

P.S. Perhaps you would be interested to know that I came up with a perfect headline for the article Will's uncle could write about you and your friends: "PU! Promiscuous Undergraduates' Sick Sex Game Stinks!"

P.P.S. Of course, right after I thought of this, it occurred to me that my headline is maybe a little too sensational for The New York Times. But I just like it so much. Luckily Will's uncle has lots of friends in the biz, so if the Times doesn't want it, perhaps we could get it in the Enquirer or the Sun, or maybe The Village Voice. . . .

*   *   *

Celeste had crumpled up the note, swallowed hard, and put her hand over her mouth to keep herself from screaming out curses right in the middle of Professor Simon's lecture on Tourette's syndrome.

The Village Voice? Jib *reads that paper.* Carla *reads that paper.* Sure, they were liberal and progressive, but even *they* had their limits. She could just imagine her parents sitting at the breakfast table with their mugs of green tea, opening the paper, seeing the headline, and having simultaneous heart attacks.

That means I'm really going to have to give Andrew my paper.

Which was so totally, horribly unfair. Celeste had been working on her essay for weeks. It was original and subversive, yet her theory was based on sound research and classic concepts. Her paper was well written, flawlessly footnoted, and a full twenty pages long (and she hadn't even had to use one of the cheat fonts!). Celeste could honestly say that it was the best paper she'd ever written. No, scratch that, it was the best paper that anyone had ever written (at least in an undergraduate psych class). The thought that Elbows was going to get credit for it combined with the fact that she had to write a new twenty-page paper was almost too much to handle.

Celeste was almost at the door of Maize Hall when she heard her name being called out. She turned and saw Artha running up to her, breathless.

"Are you okay?" she asked him. He was bent over, panting,

but he nodded. When he'd cooled off, he stood up straight and met her gaze.

"You're the one I'm worried about," he said. "I saw you run out of psych, and I've been trying to track you down—what on earth put you in such a tizzy?"

Her eyes welled up with tears, but she blinked them back. She bit her lip, wondering what to do. The AHUL was top secret, from everyone. At least, it was supposed to be. She couldn't tell Artha what was wrong. But this was a desperate situation, and her roommates didn't seem to get that. And maybe Artha *could* help her.

She leaned against the brick wall, exhaling deeply. "This is going to sound crazy to you," she began, "but that guy in our psych class, Andrew? He's blackmailing me. I have to let him turn in the paper *I* wrote, and now I have less than twenty-four hours to write a brand-new one for myself."

Artha's eyes widened. "Ex*cuse* me? What could that creep possibly have on you? You give new meaning to squeaky clean, girl."

Celeste winced. "That's—that's not exactly true." Okay, it was now or never. Celeste cast a quick glance around to make sure no one else was in earshot, then dove right in. "My roommates and I, we have this list. It's called the Alphabetical Hookup List. See, we're in a contest to see who can kiss a guy for every letter of the alphabet—in order—first. The losers have to take the winner out to dinner in Atlanta. And you know, I'm not even *playing* anymore because I lied about kissing a pregnant professor—I mean, a professor with a pregnant wife—and I just couldn't take it anymore, so I quit. But then—" She broke off, realizing that Artha was staring at her like she was from another planet.

"No, it's okay, I'm just trying to keep up," Artha assured her. "Go on."

"Well, it was all a secret, but somehow these two guys found out. And one of them's Andrew, and now he's holding it over my head and making me give him my paper—the best paper I've ever written! If I don't, his friend says he'll call his uncle who works for *The New York Times* and then everyone, everywhere, will know what we did."

Artha tilted his head in sympathy. "That's terrible," he said. "You were just having a little fun! I think the list sounds like a great idea."

Celeste sighed. "Thanks, but I have a feeling a lot of people out there would disagree."

"I guess you're right," Artha said. "There is a tinge of the unenlightened going around this campus."

"So what should I do?" Celeste asked him, her eyes filling up again. She blinked furiously.

Artha narrowed his eyes into a squint. "I think we need another brain on this one," he said. "I bet Jojo would have some ideas on how to stop these putzes. Is it okay if I tell him?"

Celeste paused, then finally nodded. What did it matter at this point, anyway?

"Good. So here's what you're going to do—you're going to go upstairs and start writing that replacement paper because the clock's ticking. And tomorrow you and me and Jordan will put our heads together and come up with a plan. Okay?"

"Mm-hmm," Celeste said. She couldn't manage much more than that without bursting into tears right there. But Artha had a point—the clock was ticking, and she was losing valuable research time.

17

Finally it was time for Ali's first book club meeting. She'd reserved a "talking" room in the back of the library, and she'd gotten there early and arranged all the chairs in a circle. She couldn't wait to see who showed up. She had a very good feeling that a Rodrigo or a Ranjan was going to be arriving any minute.

"Uh, hi, is this the book group?"

Ali tried not to let her well-rehearsed welcome-to-my-book-group grin fade when she saw the guy standing in the doorway. The scrawny, pimple-faced dude clutching an overstuffed backpack wasn't exactly what she'd been expecting. But then again, maybe he was her *R*. Maybe he was going to lead her out of the Rachmaminov/Roger/Ragner desert and into the sweet oasis of Seans and Scotts and Steves.

"Yes," Ali said. "This is the book group. My name is Ali." She stuck out her hand. "What's yours?"

"Well, Ali, my name is Rig." He glanced down at her still outstretched hand. "Um, I hope you won't be offended if I don't shake your hand. But I'm especially prone to catching colds this time of year, you see. My mucous membranes are very sensitive, and so I'm often afflicted with postnasal drip. I've just recently sneezed all over my hands and I did not have my handkerchief handy, and so it would probably be in your best interest to . . ."

Rig continued babbling, but Ali totally tuned him out. *Hooray! I found my R!* Rig's snot talk wasn't really a turn-on, but he was the first *R* boy she'd even been in the same room with since she'd finished her *Q*. And that had been *days* ago!

"And then on Wednesday, it was sort of a greenish-brown color. Kind of a cross between . . ."

Horribly revolting or not, this guy may be my only chance!

"And then on Thursday, I slept with the window open, and so it was more of a yellowish . . ."

Dude, I think the best way to go about this is get into tequila-shot-kiss mode—I should just close my eyes, open my mouth, and get this over with as quickly as possible.

Ali squeezed her eyes tight and started to lean in. *Please don't let him sneeze on me, please don't let him sneeze on me, please don't let him—*

Ali was about half a centimeter away from Rig's phlegmy face when she heard someone walk in the room. "Hey, Lee," the new guy greeted sneeze boy.

Ali snapped her eyes open and pulled back. A shiny-looking guy with a bowl cut was standing in front of her, grinning. "Wow," he said. He glanced at Ali and then back at Rig. "You were definitely right—this book group is the ideal setting for meeting some lovely specimens of the fairer sex." He turned to Ali and waggled his eyebrows. "Hello there, young lady."

"Wait. I thought you said your name was Rig?" Ali said suspiciously. Did *any* guy on this campus actually use his real name?

"Well, yeah. It's short for Wrigley. *W-r-i-g-l-e-y.* Most people call me Rig. But recently I've started calling myself Lee. I think it's quite debonair, don't you?"

Dude! I can't believe I was half a second away from kissing snot boy. And he's not even an R!

Well, at least she'd been saved in time. Now hopefully her luck would hold out and a gorgeous, charming guy named Reinhold would walk in the door next. But as the rest of the book group showed up, Ali couldn't help but be disappointed. Out of the lot of them, Wrigley just might be the most appealing. Three of them had mullets (clearly accidental, *not* fashion mullets), two wore Star Trek T-shirts, and one was picking at a scab on his elbow and appeared to be— *gross!*—eating the pieces.

Ali started the group by having everyone introduce themselves. There was a Scott, a Stephen,[29] and a Ted. There was even a Wayne. But no Robert, Richard, or Russ. It was bizarre. How could Ali have gone so many days without coming across a single guy whose name started with *R?* Wasn't that, like, one of the most commonly used letters in the whole alphabet?

□□□□□□□□□□□□□□□□□□□□□□□□□□□□□

29 If Ali had kissed him, she would have written him down on the list as Scab-Eater Stephen.

Actually, Ali was kind of relieved that she wasn't going to have to kiss any of the guys in here. And she was also kind of excited. Even if her book club wasn't full of the cutest guys, *Lady Chatterley's Lover* was pretty fucking awesome. Plus there was something sort of sweet about the way all these dorks were sitting there, looking so attentive, holding their copies of the novel.

But Ali's joy quickly faded when another guy sauntered through the door and shut it behind him. This guy was much cuter than everyone else already assembled there. But he also had a yellow-and-red tattoo of a guitar on his arm.

Will.

Great. So he was going to pull the same stupid intimidation act that Elbows had pulled with Celeste in her psych class the other day. Well, Ali refused to give Will the satisfaction of acting upset. "Welcome to the book group," she greeted him in a perfectly calm tone. "Why don't you take out your book? We were just about to get started."

He didn't even have the book with him, and he didn't pay attention. Every time Ali posed a question to the group, he would start disruptively talking to people, especially the two girls in the group. They had been sitting together, and he actually made one of them get up and move one seat over so he could sit in between them. What a sleazebag!

Ali didn't really know what to do. She didn't want to disrupt the meeting further by confronting him, so she decided to wait until it was over.

After the meeting she waited for the girls to give him their phone numbers and then, when they had gone their giggling ways, she did it. "I don't want you in this group," she said.

Will just laughed.

"I'm serious. Don't come back here next week."

"Well, Ali," he said. "I don't really see how you're in any position to ask me to do anything."

"Why are you even here?" Ali asked.

"I'm covering your book club for the *Pollard Spectator*," Will said ominously. "And there might be another story I'm writing for them involving you. And your friends."

Ali felt her neck start to get hot. "Just leave us alone," she said.

Will took his cell phone out of his pocket and dialed a number. "Hello, Uncle John, it's me, Will. Remember how I told you I might have an interesting story for you on what goes on around college campuses these days? Well, I just want you to know, I'm compiling all the data, and it's really coming along. Hope everything's okay in New York. Give me a call when you can. Bye."

Ali's jaw clenched up. She was ready to punch this asshole.

"So, as I was saying," he said to Ali when he finally hung up his stupid cell phone, "you're not exactly in any position to ask me anything, but I, on the other hand, have a favor to ask of you."

"Dude, you've got to be kidding," Ali said.

"No, dude, I'm most definitely not kidding. I was thinking that since you and your friends seem to be a bunch of cock-teases who won't give out anything more than a few lame smooches, I've decided I want you to set me up with a girl. Some hot chick who's ready to go . . ."

Ali felt a wave of dread. Celeste had been right. These guys *were* serious about the blackmail. And what was she supposed to do, let him spread their story? But how was she going to deal with Will's request? Did she even know anyone she hated enough to set up with this shithead? The idea of touching him made her want to puke.

". . . and just make sure she's got some titties on her," Will was saying. He glanced at Ali's chest. "I am definitely *not* into that whole waif thing." And then he turned on his heel and walked away.

Ali gritted her teeth and held her hands behind her back to keep from reaching out and punching him in the back of his stupid head. Then she sat down in her chair, totally defeated. The whole thing was so depressing. She had to do something to make herself feel better.

Ali went to the pay phone in the hall and took the folded wedding flyer out of her back pocket. What the hell! If nothing else, it would be a hilarious story to tell Celeste and Jodi. She unfolded the flyer and dialed the number. A girl answered, and Ali noticed she had a thick accent. Something European sounding, but she couldn't place it.

"Hello? May I please speak to Ileana?"

"I am Ileana."

"Oh. Um, hi, Ileana, my name is Ali Sheppard, and I'm calling about the ad for a wedding band. I have a great band called The Lady Chatterleys, and we'd be willing to give you a special price of five hundred dollars. I mean, even though that's less than we usually charge. So, what exactly are you looking for?" Ali curled the phone cord around her finger as she waited, glancing nervously at everyone who walked by as if someone might stop, grab the phone, and warn Ileana that her band was a fraud.

"Well, my much-loving fiancé, Melvin, and I be having very happy wedding next week," Ileana explained in somewhat broken English. "Very happy."

"I see," Ali said.

"Very in love," Ileana added. "So much romantic. We will be forever together."

I get the picture, Ali thought. This chick was a little over the top.

"And we are want a *different* band for very happy wedding."

"Oh, we're different, all right," Ali assured her. "The Lady Chatterleys are a very unusual band." It was all she could do to keep from cracking up.

"I like name of the band," Ileana said.

"So, do you want us to audition or something?"

"Do you have CD?" Ileana asked.

Ali practically choked. A CD! They had never even sung one single song.

"No, it's still being mastered, uh, in the studio," Ali said. This was fucking hilarious!

"Well, okay, you are hired," Ileana said. She gave Ali the date and time. After the ceremony in the chapel, the "reception" would be held at a frat house.

Now that's class, Ali thought. *Who needs the Atlanta Four Seasons when you've got frat houses? And The Lady Chatterleys to boot.*

This would definitely cheer Jodi and Celeste up after she told them what had happened with Will.

But she wasn't going to take this gag any farther. She'd call Ileana in a day or so and tell her that they couldn't do her "gig." It wouldn't be right to ruin someone's wedding just to get five hundred dollars. Would it?

18

Jodi looked at her newly acquired wad of one-dollar bills and smiled. *I must be a* really *good kisser,* she thought happily. *But does the fact that I just got paid for kissing make me some sort of prostitute?*

Lance had given her a twelve-dollar tip. *Twelve dollars* on a ten-dollar cab ride. And Jodi could certainly use the money. Just as she was thinking about whether her twelve dollars would best be spent on new mascara or a hundred and twenty nasty beers at Dimers, the radio crackled on.

"Love Bug. Come in, Love Bug," Dakota's voice came through the radio. "Listen, girl, I don't know what kind of magic spells or pheromones or whatever that shit is that you're putting out there . . . but today is your lucky day. I know this was supposed to be your last ride, but check this out—fella comes in here just now and asks for you, specifically. Cute fella, too. And I said, 'Well, Jodi's not going to be driving here anymore.' And then he says, 'But it's really important. I need to see her. I think she'll change her mind when she sees me.' Didn't even say where he needed to go. And between you and me, I think he might be sweet on you. But that's just Dakota's opinion."

"A cute fella—I mean, guy—asked for me?" Jodi yelled into the broken radio. "Who? Who was it? Did he say his name?" But all she heard in response was Dakota humming.

Although she didn't want to let herself get too excited, the cute guy had to be Zack. After all, they hadn't spoken even once since that terrible scene in his dorm. And by now he'd probably realized that he liked her too much to let something so stupid get in the way of their being together.

I wonder how he found out I'm working here? Clearly he went to a lot of trouble. Oh, that is just so sweet.

Jodi pulled into the taxi station's parking lot, smiled at herself in the rearview mirror, and got out of the car. She imagined how cute he'd look standing in the waiting area, all apologetic. He'd probably be holding a bouquet of flowers. No, wait, not flowers. Flowers were too conventional. Maybe he'd bring her something odd but touching, like a bouquet of radishes.

And then after we make up, we'll get in the cab and drive somewhere secluded and get in the backseat and mmmm . . .

Jodi walked through the door and, in the space of about

two seconds, went from being really, really excited to being absolutely fucking crushed.

It wasn't Zack who she saw standing there waiting for her. It was Lucas—or rather, Will. And he wasn't alone—some other guy was with him. Probably Celeste's would-be rapist, Andrew.

What the fuck?

"Hey there, Jodi, so good to see you." Will smiled.

"This nice woman told us you weren't going to work here anymore," Andrew said. "But we had a feeling that you'd make an exception when you saw us."

Oh, God. Celeste was right—these guys aren't going to let it drop.

"By the way, I'm sorry about that thing at Casino Night. Guess I messed things up pretty good for you and your boyfriend." Will smiled insincerely.

"Hey, Love Bug," Dakota called her over to the cage. "The other one showed up after I called you," she explained with a wink. "Two boys—you really are something! You know, we usually reserve it for our fancy business clients, but since I'm in a good mood today and this does seem to be a special occasion, I'm going to let you take the Buick!" And before Jodi could protest, Dakota winked at her again and handed her a set of keys.

"Have fun, you three," Dakota said, grinning. "Don't do anything I wouldn't do."

Eeew.

Jodi reluctantly led Will and Andrew out to the cab.

"Oh, by the way," Andrew said. "It looks like we don't have any money, so you're going to have to foot the bill for this one."

"No fucking way," Jodi spat out.

"Don't worry," Will said. "We'll pay you back soon. My birthday's coming up, and my *uncle* usually sends me a check."

Jodi couldn't believe it. Not only did she have to drive them wherever the hell they wanted to go, but she was actually going to lose money doing so. With the money from Lance, she'd be lucky if she broke even.

"Fine. Get in the car." Jodi unlocked the door to the 1987 Buick and got in.

Will put his hands on his hips. "Well! Andrew, I'm astonished! Our cabbie hasn't even opened the door for us!"

"Oh, my word! You're right. This is unacceptable," Andrew said in the same mock-horrified tone.

Jodi felt her face grow hot. This was just too humiliating. She went around to the backseat and opened the door. Will got in, and then Andrew did, and it took heroic effort to resist slamming the door on his foot.

Jodi got in the front. "Fine, where the fuck are we going?"

"Now, now, no need to be cranky," Will said condescendingly. "Actually, we've made a list of places we'd like to go." He passed her a piece of paper.

Jodi looked at the list and groaned. They wanted her to

take them everywhere from the Accordion Pavilion to Zena's Xerox Town.

"There are twenty-six places on that list, all in alphabetical order!" Andrew said gleefully.

"Get it? Alphabetical! Like your list!" Will said. And then they both cracked up like this was the best joke they'd ever heard.

19

It was a weird evening in the triple. Ali and Celeste were both there, but the room was virtually silent. There was no giggling, no drinking, and although a new episode of *The Osbournes* was on in the lounge, they weren't on their way down to watch it.

Instead Celeste was sitting at her desk, typing frantically. Ali was alternately reading *Lady Chatterley's Lover* and scribbling on a pad labeled with the heading "Girls to Set Up with That Asshole Will."[30] Every so often one of them would shout out, "Fuck Picks," or "Fuck Elbows," or sometimes just "Fucking fuck fuck."

Ali was mid-*f*-word when Jodi walked in, slammed the door, threw her backpack on the ground, and shouted, "I am going to kill them. I swear to God, I am going to fucking kill them."

"Dude," Ali said, putting down her pad. "Where have you

---

30 Ali hadn't written down any names yet, but she'd drawn a lovely picture of a dancing teakettle.

been? It's seven o'clock at night, and I thought you were quitting your job today."

"And what's with your shirt?" Celeste asked, looking up just long enough to realize that Jodi's sweater was covered in giant brown chunks.

"You will not *believe* what happened to me today," Jodi said. "This . . ." She pointed to one of the chunks on her shirt. "This," Jodi said, louder, almost yelling, "is a piece of *meatball*. I have a fucking *meatball* stuck to my fucking *shirt*. And do you know *why* I have a meatball stuck to my fucking shirt? Elbows and Picks!" Jodi paused, took a deep breath, then quickly explained what the two guys had pulled on her. "And *then*, after hours and hours, when we got up to *Y*, they made me drive them to Yummy's Sandwich Bonanza and they both got these big-ass stinky meatball subs. And they got sauce all over the back of the cab, and because I was driving the special-occasion Buick, I had to clean it up!" Jodi threw herself facedown on her bed and punched her pillow. "Aaaaaaaaaaaaggghh!"

"Well, dude," Ali sighed. "Elbows and Picks were pretty busy today. Celeste and I *both* had visits from them." Celeste and Ali told Jodi about their respective forms of blackmail.

"It's the best paper I have ever written in my entire life," Celeste said, her eyes getting teary. "There's a colon, right there in the heading! I've never written a paper with a colon in the heading before."

"And okay," Ali jumped in, "so I know I said I would fix Will up with someone. But the more I think about it, the more I think that no one, *no one* deserves to be fixed up with either of those shitheads." Ali tore the piece of paper off her pad and crumpled it up. Then she uncrumpled it. "But I've got to find someone," she muttered.

"Celeste," Jodi said. "I am *so* sorry that we ever thought that you were being silly for worrying about this. You were right—this is a big deal. This is a big fucking deal. What are we going to do?" She looked up at her roommates. Celeste was leafing through a book with one hand and tapping a pencil against the desk with the other. Ali was tearing sheets off her pad and crumpling them up one by one.

"Hello?" Jodi said. "You guys! We have to do something about this. This is fucked up."

"I know," Celeste said. "This is beyond awful. And we still haven't thought of a way to stop them. Although . . ." She paused, wondering if her roommates would kill her when she revealed the fact that she'd shared their secret with someone willingly. Maybe they'd be happy that Artha was going to help, though. She pressed her lips together, trying to decide what to do.

"I was actually thinking about going to visit Milton tomorrow at the hospital," Ali offered before Celeste could make up her mind. "Maybe he'll have some suggestions. He knows about this kind of stuff, right?"

"That's a good idea," Jodi said.

Celeste nodded. She looked back at her computer screen, overwhelmed by how much work she still had to do. Maybe it was better not to mention the Artha thing after all—she didn't have time for a fight, and she'd definitely be risking one. "I am *never* going to finish this," she muttered. "It is not humanly possible."

"Yeah. So then there's nothing to worry about," Ali said, without sounding too convinced. "It'll be fine, dudes. Just fine."

But none of them were convinced.

20

For the first time in her life, Celeste Alexander was going to be late to class. She'd been up all night, trying to write something even one-tenth as good as her last paper, but she just couldn't do it. Finally at two in the morning she'd come up with a stupid, boring, incredibly lame topic (Fromm was so passé). And not only had she been forced to use the Courier New font, but she'd put also had to switch to thirteen-point type (instead of the regular twelve point) and to double-and-a-half-space the paper. Even then it was only eighteen pages. Celeste raced to the psych building. Ever since she'd met Andrew, she'd been doing a lot of running. *What a great new exercise program!* Had she been in a better mood, had she gotten more than two hours of sleep, Celeste might have giggled at this thought, but after the twenty-four hours she'd just had, a wry smile was all she could muster.

By the time Celeste got to the classroom, she was fifteen minutes late. She snuck in as quietly as she could and dropped the two papers, almost forty typed pages, into the basket on Professor Simon's desk. As Celeste was looking for a seat, she spotted Andrew giving her his disgusting smile. He winked. Celeste was actually in the process of putting up her hand up to give him the finger,[31] but just at that second Professor Simon glanced over and gave her a look of disappointment (luckily, for the first time in her life, she was too tired to care).

She walked to the back row, collapsed into the only available seat, and immediately fell asleep. She finally woke up at the end of class when Artha Stewart tapped her on the shoulder.

"Jordan's meeting us outside class," he told her. "We're going to take you out for some good girl talk and figure out a way to stop these two jerk-offs from ruining your life, okay?"

Great. She didn't know whether to laugh or cry. But maybe it would be nice to go out with them and try to get her mind off the fact that she'd just turned in the worst paper of her entire academic career.

□□□□□□□□□□□□□□□□□□□□□□□□□□□□□□□□

31 This would also have been the first time in her entire life that Celeste had done this. She was a bird-flipping virgin.

21

Ali pushed open the heavy glass doors of the Sydney Markus Memorial Hospital, walked inside, and smiled.

Ah, memories.

Hospitals didn't make Ali think of death and sickness, as they did with most people. They didn't make her sad either, just nostalgic for her junior year in high school and a guy she'd dated at the time, Paul Julian. Back when she was sixteen, Ali had gone through a revolutionary-outlaw phase, which had consisted of listening exclusively to Bob Dylan music and never taking off her favorite Fred Hampton Lives! T-shirt. (She didn't know who Fred Hampton was, but she'd gotten the shirt from the Revolution Solution store at the mall, so she knew it meant something important.) When she first met Paul, she was really excited. He fit in perfectly with her new life! He had lots of strong political beliefs (Ali was never quite sure what these were exactly), he hated "The Man," and he wouldn't listen to any music recorded after 1975. While they were dating, he even came up with this idea that it would be really cool if he found a way to steal a lot of pharmaceuticals from the local hospital.[32] He figured there had to be some main drug-supply closet (he knew this from watching *ER*), but he had no idea where it might be located. So he spent a lot of his free time wandering through the corridors of Atlanta General in search of "the good shit." And while he never did find any morphine or Percoset, he happened to stumble upon a room where a lot of the medical equipment was stored. And it was from there that Paul got (i.e., stole) most of the presents he'd given Ali during their ten-week relationship. Once it was a box of latex gloves (almost two-thirds full), another time a pair of forceps (never used), and for Valentine's Day it was one of those blue-paper gowns (which Ali had ended up wearing as a dress).

Being in hospitals always made Ali think fondly of Paul and the nice times they'd had before he dumped her for a candy striper.[33]

Ali walked down the long white hallway to the giant information desk, where a stern-looking woman was sitting behind a little plastic sign that read, AMANDA JUGGERTON: COMPUTER INFORMATION SYSTEMS COORDINATOR.

"Hello," Ali said.

Amanda Juggerton looked up. She had the most enormous breasts Ali had ever seen in her entire life.

"Can I help you?" she asked in an irritated voice.

Dude, Ali thought, starting to giggle. *I can't believe her last name is* actually *Juggerton.*

---

32 This idea was born one night after Ali and Paul had gotten high and watched *Drugstore Cowboy,* a movie (starring Matt Dillon) about a gang of perscription drug thieves.

33 Or, as Ali liked to call her, "the Candy Stripper," which isn't actually a very good insult, but it was the best she could think of at the time.

"Can I help you?" Amanda Juggerton said again.

Amanda Juggerton of the Gigantic Jugs . . . Ali put her hand over her mouth, trying desperately to stop giggling.

"Can . . . I . . . help . . . you?" Amanda Juggerton repeated slowly, overpronouncing each word as if talking to someone who didn't speak English.

Ali's giggle turned into a full-blown laugh. She didn't mean to be rude, but the more she thought about it, the funnier it seemed. *God, I can't wait to tell Jodi and Celeste about this.*

"Is there something about a hospital full of sick people that you find particularly amusing, young lady?"

"No. Sorry. It's just that your name . . . ha ha . . . it . . . ha ha . . . makes you sound like a *porn star*," Ali said.

Amanda Juggerton narrowed her eyes.

"Are you here for some sort of purpose?"

"Yeah. I'm here to visit Milton Copley. He fell off a roof."

Amanda Juggerton typed something into the computer. "Floor four, room number eleven. And please try not to disturb anyone."

What is it about hospitals that makes everyone so cranky? Ali wondered as she walked away from the desk and into the elevator. *Jugs, Juggerton—come on! It's funny!*

She rode the elevator up to the fourth floor, got out, and walked down the corridor. Room eight, nine, ten . . . There was a man standing right in front of room eleven. He was wearing a white lab coat and holding a clipboard, and he had a stethoscope around his neck. With his curly blond hair and smooth-shaven face, Ali thought he looked just like one of those I'm-not-really-but-I-play-one-on-TV doctors, or else Doogie Howser.

"What's up, Doc?" Ali said. "I'm here to see Milton Copley. Is it okay for me to go in there?"

"Yes, of course." He smiled. His teeth were very white, almost freakishly so. "I'm the physician attending Mr. Copley."

"Hi. I'm Ali." She stuck out her hand. Ali always felt very adult shaking hands when she met people. *I wonder what his name is. Kissing a doctor in a hospital, that would be pretty hot.* And maybe now that she was off campus she could finally find a freaking *R*.

"I'm Dr. Frank Pembrook," he said as he put out his hand and shook Ali's.

Shit, not an R, Ali thought. *Oh, well. It would probably distract me from my mission, anyway. And it really is a very important mission that I'm on.*

"Are you a relative of Mr. Copley's?" Dr. Pembrook asked.

"No, I used to be his assistant." Ali loved it when she was given the opportunity to talk about working for Milton. Sure, she had pretty much just been his secretary, but she always told people she was an assistant private investigator. It just sounded so much *cooler.*

Doctor Pembrook smiled again. "Well, then you'll be happy to know I just looked at your boss here and he's doing very well. He's quite a character, you know."

Ali nodded. Milton was pretty cool. He had to be at least

sixty-five years old, but he was always doing risky and exciting things for his stakeouts. He talked like an old-time detective and he didn't even get mad when she sometimes forgot to give him his phone messages. He would just smirk, say something about "broads" or "dames," and leave it at that. And to think Ali had met him totally by accident while she was applying for a waitressing job.

"I was in there dropping off Mr. Copley's X rays. He's healing nicely." Dr. Pembrook held open the door and Ali walked in.

When she first saw Milton she gasped, not sure whether to laugh or cry. On the one hand, the accident was clearly worse than she'd originally thought: His right leg was in a giant cast, held up in a sling. His left arm was sticking straight out to the side at a ninety-degree angle, also covered in a cast and propped up by a set of metal rods. Yet despite this Milton had clearly made himself right at home in the little white room. His typewriter was set up on the small night table next to the bed, with piles of white paper scattered all around on the floor. Next to the table there was a chair with his forties-style trench coat thrown over the back, and his telephoto-lens camera was laid out on the seat. At the foot of his bed was the giant four-reel recorder that he used to tape telephone conversations. With his good arm he was holding a pair of old-fashioned binoculars up to his eyes—they were pointed toward the window. He was wearing a fedora.

"Hey, dude," Ali said cheerily.

"Grrrmph," Milton said. He put the binoculars down and looked at Ali.

"I'm so sorry about your accident. I can't believe you fell off a roof. That really sucks."

"Mmmmmrf!" Milton said, louder.

Oh my God, what is that?! There was a trail of bright red splotches on the front of Milton's gown. The splotches were glossy and wet looking.

"Milton!" Ali shrieked. "You're bleeding. Oh my God, I'll go find Dr. Pembrook."

"Grrrp. Mrrrrp!" Milton waved his good arm around over his head. He pointed to the stains on the gown, and then he pointed to a doughnut box on the floor containing a dozen deflated jelly doughnuts.

Phew. It was only jelly—not blood. *I wonder why he's only eating the jelly part?* Ali thought this was a little odd, but then again, Milton was kind of an odd guy.

"Hey, look. I brought you a present. Sorry about the shitty wrapping job," she said, handing Milton a medium-sized rectangular package covered in a Pollard book cover. She had crossed out the Pollard crest and written *Get Well Soon* in big letters.

Milton unwrapped it and held up a white cardboard box. In big red letters it read, *Aunt Biggly's Saltwater Taffy: An Authentic Taste of the Boardwalk.*

"Gggrrrmmp!" Milton said excitedly.

"I don't understand," Ali said. "Why do you keep making those funny noises?"

Milton waved his arm around again and started pointing at the clipboard attached to the foot of the bed. He waved his arm, and Ali handed it to him.

The piece of paper attached to the clipboard was full of diagrams and scribbles and very official-looking medical words. Ali read the line that Milton was pointing to:

Occlusion set in position as existed prior to accident to aid in proper healing.

"Dude," Ali said. "You just totally lost me."

"Mmmf wwwwrd mmm jmmm sssmmmmm." Milton pointed to his mouth.

"Huh?"

"Mmmf wwwrd mmm jmmm sssmmmm!" Milton pulled back his lips, revealing a row of shiny metal braces.

"Oooh," Ali said. "I get it, *they wired your jaw shut.* Fuck, so I guess this maybe wasn't the best idea for a present, huh. Oops, sorry." Ali looked at Milton. He shrugged.

Ali shrugged back, then sank into the plastic visitor's chair next to his bed. "I'm in trouble and I really need your help," she said. "I hate to bother you when you're in the hospital and all that, but . . ."

With his good arm Milton grabbed a pad and a pen off the night table and scribbled something furiously. He handed it to Ali.

Don't worry, it said. "Grrrmph," he grunted. He wrote some more: *So what's the trouble?*

"Well, it's really bad. See, my roommates and I, we're

being blackmailed by this stupid guy Elbows and his stupid friend Picks, who has an uncle who works for *The New York Times,* so if he wanted to, he could really tell a fuckload of people what we did."

Milton started writing again.

"Please, please don't ask me what we did. I really can't tell you. But—"

Milton held up his hand and nodded. He ripped off the piece of paper he'd been writing on, crumpled it up, and threw it on the floor. Then he wrote something on a new piece of paper and held it up.

Two words: blackmail back.

Blackmail back. It sounded simple enough. . . .

"How, exactly?"

Milton started writing again: *Pull the old switcheroo.*

"Huh?" Ali said. "What's 'the old switcheroo'?"

Right now they're the ones in control, but that's just because they have something on you. Find their weaknesses. Get something on them.

Suddenly Ali felt much better. *It can't be that hard to think of something.*

She clapped her hands together and grinned.

"Thanks so much, dude. You're the best." She leaned over and kissed Milton on the cheek. "Really, I mean it. If you ever need any help with any assignments, like, you need someone to go with you on a stakeout or something, you know where to find me!"

"Ggggrrp," Milton said.

Ali walked toward the door. Just as she was opening it, a crumpled piece of paper bounced off her head.

Good luck, Ali. You're a fine-looking broad. If I were forty years younger and you dressed more like a dame, I think we'd make quite a pair.

Ali smiled. She knew the message was a little bit icky and maybe should have grossed her out. But actually, she thought it was sort of sweet.

22

Celeste gazed around the very tacky Pins and Stripes bowling alley, where Jordan and Artha had brought her for some distraction after their "girl talk" coffee outing, during which Celeste had filled them both in on the latest events. Artha had taken bowling as his phys ed requirement, and the professor had told him that if he didn't knock down at least one pin by the end of the semester, he would fail.

Bowling was pretty much Celeste's least-favorite thing, especially when it was combined with her other least-favorite thing—lazy-eyed, narcoleptic K. J. Martin, who was bowling a few lanes down with a smaller clone of herself. At least lazy-eyed, narcoleptic K. J. was bowling. Her little sister had dozed off on the bench and was snoring loudly. Lazy-eyed, narcoleptic K. J. Martin waved vigorously at Celeste, and Celeste gave a little wave back.

"Why do we have to be here?" Celeste asked, for the fourteenth time.

"I told you, I have to practice," Artha said.

"But did you have to wear that?" Jordan asked.

Artha was dressed in full bowling regalia: tight light-green-and-white-checked pedal pushers and a pink bowling shirt with the name *Bruce* stitched on the pocket.

"I thought maybe it would help me get into the whole spirit of the thing. The Pins and Stripes spirit," Artha said.

"But why the name *Bruce*?" Jordan asked.

"I thought that sounded more bowly, you know, more masculine."

"You thought the name *Bruce* sounded masculine?" Celeste asked, laughing. "Even *Artha* sounds more masculine than *Bruce*."

"Well, I like it," Artha said, picking up a ball from the rack. Then he picked up another one. "These are my two lucky balls," he said.

Celeste and Jordan looked at each other and laughed. This was fun. Even though her life pretty much sucked, thanks to Andrew the Asshole, at least she was having a good time right now. It was pretty hard to bowl on two hours of sleep, though. Especially since Celeste couldn't bowl even when fully rested.

Artha bowled a gutter ball and dramatically threw up his hands in frustration.

"Maybe you should try a sport that's a little more low-key," Jordan said, giving him a loving shoulder-squeeze. "Like pick-up sticks."

He and Celeste shared a knowing look.[34]

□□□□□□□□□□□□□□□□□□□□□□□□□□□□□□□

34 You have to read book one (A→J) to get this.

"Pick-up sticks?" Artha asked. "What's that?"

"Nothing. It's an inside thing with me and Celeste," Jordan said.

Artha bowled again, but this time the ball was so far off course, it bounced all the way over to lazy-eyed, narcoleptic K. J. Martin's lane and knocked down two of her pins. "I hit some! I hit some!" Artha said, jumping up and down. He wrote a two with his little minipencil on the scorecard. Lazy-eyed, narcoleptic K. J. Martin and her little sister didn't even notice, because they were both sprawled out in their seats, sound asleep.

"I think you have to knock down the pins in your own lane in order to count them," Celeste said.

"Okay, fine, whatever," Artha said, ignoring her and rolling a gutter ball. They all stood and watched the ball slowly, noisily creep down the gutter and get stuck. A lane guy had to come and get the ball. He scowled at them and suggested they try the kids' lane, which had rubber padding instead of gutters, so you pretty much had to knock at least one pin down with every ball.

"So listen," Artha said, putting his hands on his hips. "Let's not forget what our mission here today is—coming up with a good revenge plan for these little weasels who are bullying you and your friends. I think the first thing we have to do is come up with a name for the plan."

"No, the first thing we have to do is get some nachos and hamburgers," Jordan said.

"And some fries," Celeste piped in.

They ordered, and then Artha brought up the name thing again.

"What do you mean, come up with a name?" Celeste asked.

"You know, like Operation Desert Storm," Artha said.

For some reason, the seriousness with which Artha said the words *Operation Desert Storm* made Celeste and Jordan laugh so hard, they had to bend over and put their heads between their knees. Celeste really liked Jordan. Normally if she had been rejected by a guy the way she had been rejected by Jordan, it would have been very hard for her to be friends with him. But there was something about the fact that he had really become so openly gay that made all the bad feelings disappear.

"I don't see what's so damn funny. How about Operation . . ." Artha couldn't think of anything. "It should be something with AHUL in it. Like Operation Alphabetical Hack-Up List. I know— Operation Annihilate, Hack Up, and Leave. What, you don't like that?" Artha said when he saw their unimpressed faces. "Then you come up with something."

"How about Mission Impossible?" Celeste said sadly. How were they supposed to scare these guys off if all they could do was sit around and come up with moronic names?

Sometimes things were just beyond your grasp. Like, for instance, that morning her father, Jib, had called her, all excited because he had read in the paper that regular people were getting to go to the moon and you just had to get on some list and pay a lot of money. "We're going to go to the moon, you and me," Jib had said.

"But Jib," Celeste had told him, "you haven't even been able to get us tickets to *The Producers* on Broadway. How are you going to get us on a shuttle to the moon?" The whole thing was ridiculous.

It was a nice thought but an impossibility, just like this little Operation Whatever of Artha and Jordan's was an impossibility. What could they really do to stop these guys from ruining her and her friends' lives?

Artha was deep in thought.[35] "You know what I hate the most about those guys? I mean, other than the fact that they're torturing you and Jodi and Ali?" he asked Celeste.

"What?" Celeste asked.

"I hate the fact that they're such fucking homophobes. I mean, they really are the type of guys who would kill someone like me for wearing this shirt." He pointed to his pink shirt.

"Well, *I* could kill you for wearing that shirt," Jordan said.

"No, I'm serious," Artha said.

"You're right, it's true," Jordan said. "I mean, they're so filled with rage, it's not funny. They're like these guys I knew in high school who—"

All of a sudden Jordan was cut off by a voice yelling, "DUDES!"

They spun around and saw Ali and Jodi running toward them. Jodi's hair was flying out in all directions, and Ali's face was bright red. "*There* you are!" Ali exclaimed, panting.

□□□□□□□□□□□□□□□□□□□□□□□□□□□□□□□□□□□□□□□
35 Jordan was deep in nachos.

She stopped for a second in front of Celeste, catching her breath, then continued. "Jodi and I wanted to meet you after class, Celeste, but I was late getting back to the dorm from meeting Milton, and you weren't there. So Jodi and I decided to get some coffee. And then the guy who worked there was cute, but his name didn't start with *R*. And then Broomie Bill[36] said that he'd seen you a while earlier and you'd gone off with Artha. And then he started saying that he 'didn't understand kids' fashion these days', and then he described what you were wearing, Artha. And then we figured out that maybe you'd be playing golf, but then Jodi was like, 'Oh, wait, we don't have a golf course at PU.' So then we figured you were dressed up for bowling. And so we ran over here . . . and here you are."

Jordan, Celeste, and Artha stared at her with their mouths hanging open.

"Are you sure you only had one cup of coffee?" Artha asked, giggling. "You *so* did not have only one cup," Jodi said, shaking her finger at Ali. "When you first got to the triple, you were so caffeinated, you were practically vibrating."

"Well, okay, fine," Ali conceded. "They were having this special deal at Bean Town, and every coffee came with an extra shot of espresso in it for no extra charge. And I know it's not your fault or anything, Celeste, but I hardly got any sleep last night, because you had to stay up and write that

□□□□□□□□□□□□□□□□□□□□□□□□□□□□□□

36 Broomie Bill—Been on the PU campus since the sixties. Knows the name of every student, past and present. Is not employed by the university but of his own accord wanders around campus all day, sweeping. The administration has never done anything about Broomie Bill, mostly due to the fact that he is very skilled with a broom.

paper because of that Elbows fucker. So I was like all, 'Sure, dudes, put that shot in there. And throw another one in while you're at it.'"

"Anyway, Celeste, we came here because we need to talk to you," Jodi said.

"Yeah, we need to talk to you about *some stuff*." Ali nodded, opening her eyes wide for emphasis.

"Ali, sweetheart, please do *not* make that face. When you do that with your eyes, you remind me of that scary dead girl in *Sixth Sense*. You will make me pee my pants," Artha said, feigning fear. Jordan rolled his eyes. Celeste giggled.

"Hello? Celeste? We need to talk to you about something *important*. In *private*." Jodi tugged gently on the end on Celeste's sleeve. "Can we talk to you *over there?*"

"Um, okay, sure." Celeste started to follow Ali and Jodi across the bowling alley.

"Ooh, are you going to talk about the AHUL?" Artha called behind them. "Can I come? I *love* talking about the AHUL. And I totally want to help with the plan."

Ali and Jodi stopped dead in their tracks and turned around.

"Wait, did you just say you *love talking about the AHUL?*" Jodi said, trying to stay calm.

"Yeah," Artha said. "Totally. I think it's a work of pure genius. Don't you agree, Jojo?' He turned to Jordan.

"Well," Jordan said. "It really is clever. And when Artha told me about those creeps trying to blackmail you, I really wanted to help somehow."

"Wait, what the fuck is going on here?" Ali demanded, turning to Celeste. "Why do they fucking know about the fucking AHUL?"

"I cannot believe you told them," Jodi said before Celeste had a chance to answer. She put her hands on her hips. "Doesn't swearing to keep something a secret mean *anything* to you? We're supposed to be your *best friends!*"

"Wait, you guys. Please try and understand," Celeste pleaded. "I only told Artha because he was with me after Elbows told me about having to give him the paper. And I was really upset and he asked and—"

"And she knew she could trust me because, I mean, look at this face! This is a face a girl can trust!" Artha said, smiling angelically.

"And we really do want to help out," Jordan said.

"I'm really sorry I didn't clear it with you guys first," Celeste said. "It's just, there's been so much messed-up stuff going on lately, and I didn't think telling them would make things any worse. And maybe it'll actually make things better, because they think those guys are total assholes and they really want to help us get back at them. And with five of us working on a plan, we're bound to come up with something good. *Please* don't be mad."

Ali and Jodi looked at each other.

"Well, I *guess* it's okay," Jodi said slowly.

"Ali?"

"Okay, fine. It's too late to take it back, anyway," Ali sighed. "But you guys have to *swear* you will not tell *anyone,*" she said, giving Jordan and Artha her sternest look.

"Yeah." Jodi nodded. "Do you guys swear? Jordan?"

"I solemnly swear to uphold the sanctity of the AHUL," Jordan said.

"Artha?"

"I swear on my new Diesel jeans, I will not tell a soul," Artha said seriously. "And if I blab to even *one* person, let me be sentenced to a lifetime of wearing nothing but cowboy boots and horizontal stripes. So help me God, I do."

"Wow, Artha," Jodi said with a laugh. "You clearly have the proper respect for the AHUL."

"Okay, good. So it's settled, then." Celeste smiled, relieved. "So Ali, Jodi, what were you coming here to tell me?"

"Okay," Ali started. "So, I talked to Milton. Or actually, I talked and he wrote me notes because of the wires. And it was funny, because I'd brought him this saltwater taffy and—"

"Ali," Jordan said gently. "You have to slow down. We have no idea what you're talking about."

"It's true, sugar pie," Artha agreed. "This stuff you're saying is making less sense than tapered pants. And nothing makes less sense than tapered pants. Like, hello? Even Ally McBeal would look big-assed in tapered pants."

"Artha, let the girl talk," Jordan said, patting Artha's shoulder.

Ali took a deep breath, then blurted out everything Milton had told her.

"So, I guess what we need to do is think of what these jerkoffs' weaknesses are," Jordan said reasonably.

"Well . . . ," Celeste said. "They seem to think every woman on campus should be in love with them. . . ."

"So there's one weakness," Jodi agreed. "They both have really big egos."

"And like we were just saying, they're total homophobes," Artha piped in.

"But how could we use that to pull the old . . . what was that thing he said we're supposed to pull?" Jordan asked.

"The old switcheroo," Ali said. "We need to somehow figure out a way to turn the tables on them, involving their weaknesses. . . ."

"Well, then," Artha said slowly. "The way I see it, it's simple."

"What is?" Celeste said.

"Operation Out," Artha said.

"What are you talking about?" Jodi asked.

"What would those two, Elbows and Picks, hate more than anything?" Artha asked.

Everyone stared blankly at him.

"Um, having to wear your green-checked pants?" Ali suggested after a long silence.

Artha gave her a patient smile. "Nice try, but . . . no." He leaned forward, eyes sparkling. "How about the entire campus thinking they're gay?"

"Oh my God, that's perfect!" Celeste said.

"Yeah," Jodi agreed. "Now we just have to figure out exactly how to do it. . . ."

23

After bowling, Celeste, Ali, and Jodi headed back to Maize Hall to get some much needed rest before putting the plan in action. Meanwhile Ali realized that with all the crazy blackmailing going on the day before, she'd totally forgotten to tell her roomies about the gig she'd scheduled for their band, and she quickly brought them up to speed on her phone conversation with Ileana.

"What!" Celeste said, horrified. "You've got to be kidding."

"No, it's great!" Ali said. "We get five hundred dollars. Dude, that's, like, over a hundred and fifty each. I'm going to sing, and Jodi's going to play trumpet. We figure you probably learned some kind of instrument at that fancy New York City high school you went to."

"Stuyvesant was not a fancy school," Celeste said defensively. "But I can play a little violin."

"That's great!" Jodi said, getting really excited. "We'll be like Nickel Creek or Dixie Chicks or The Corrs."

"I don't know who any of those people are," Celeste said,

totally confused. "I mean, I basically don't know much more than 'Twinkle, Twinkle, Little Star.'"

"You've never heard of the Dixie Chicks?" Jodi said.

"Are they like the Spice People?" Celeste asked, trying to be cool.

"It doesn't matter, that's fine, dude, we can work with that," Ali said. "You and Jodi can go to the music department tomorrow and borrow your instruments, and then we can get together and have a rehearsal."

"You're sure it's not kind of crazy?" Celeste asked. She was totally into supporting her friends, but this did sound a little strange.

"Oh, come on, we can at least try one rehearsal," Jodi said. "I mean, we're not all doing the AHUL anymore, and there has to be *something* we can all work on together."

"But there *is* something else we're all working on together," Celeste said with a smile. "Remember? Operation Out—our revenge on Picks and Elbows."

24

The next day Ali stood outside Celeste's psych classroom, her heart pounding. Operation Out was already exciting, and she hadn't even completed the first step yet! She looked at her watch. Celeste's class ended in five minutes, which meant that in five minutes Elbows would be walking out that door, right into her trap.

"Agent A-Dog preparing for stage one," Ali whispered to herself.

If she'd gotten her way, Ali would have been whispering that into a walkie-talkie. She'd suggested getting them for the mission, and Artha had even agreed with her. "That'd be so *Charlie's Angels,*" he'd said excitedly. But unfortunately, Jodi, Jordan, and Celeste hadn't thought it would make much sense.

"No part of our mission actually requires a walkie-talkie," Celeste had pointed out.

Well, even without the walkie-talkies, being involved in a secret mission was still pretty fucking cool. Even cooler was the fact that if it worked, they wouldn't have to deal with Picks or Elbows ever again.

Ali looked at her watch again. *Mission commencing in T minus four minutes.*

She took the piece of bright pink paper out of her backpack and looked it over one last time. On the outside was written *Do Not Read Unless You Are Ali* in Jodi's bubbly handwriting. And inside:

Hey Ali,

So I was thinking about what you said earlier, and even though I wasn't sure at first, I realized that I totally agree with you. There's just something so sexy about the way Andrew and Will have taken such control of the situation. I mean, I know it's kind of sick in an S-and-M way, or whatever. But . . . I mean, like, when I was driving them around in the cab, the whole time all I could think was, man, I'd sure like to get in the backseat with both those hotties. Do you think Will knew how jealous you were when he was asking you to fix him up with a girl? Oh my God, Celeste would think we were so horrible if she knew we felt this way, wouldn't she? We have to make sure she doesn't find out. And I have to try and stop fantasizing about those guys! Okay, I'll see you later at home.

XOXO,
Jodi

It was perfect.

Ali refolded the note and stuck it in between the pages of her notebook. And then she looked at her watch again. Just as she looked back up, the door opened and people started streaming out of the classroom. She spotted Andrew doing that stupid cocky walk of his. *That fucker has no idea who he's messing with,* Ali thought with a smirk. She waved at Celeste.

"Hey, Celeste," Ali shouted loudly. "Over here!"

"Oh, hi, Ali," Celeste called back. Ali continued in Celeste's direction, keeping Andrew in her peripheral vision. And then at the perfect moment she "tripped," tumbling forward and throwing everything she was carrying to the ground.

"FUCK!" she screamed loudly. "I've dropped all my stuff!" *Was that too much? Did it sound fake?* Apparently not, because as Andrew walked by, she saw him watching her bend over to pick up her stuff. She quickly gathered up everything except for the bright pink note.

"Oh, Ali, you're such a klutz sometimes," Celeste giggled. "Come on, let's go to the dining hall." Ali and Celeste continued walking very slowly. They both really wanted to turn around and see what was happening behind them. (If they had, they would have seen Andrew walk up to the note. Look left. Look right. Bend down and pick it up quickly. Look left. Look right. Stuff it in his pocket and walk away.)

Ali glanced over to the water fountain, where Jordan had been hanging out, watching the whole thing.

He gave her a thumbs-up.

Ali smiled. *Stage one complete.*

25

After the successful completion of stage one, everyone went their separate ways, and Ali decided that now would be a good time to work on her own personal mission: Operation Where the Hell Is My *R*. It was fucked up, totally fucking *fucked up* how much trouble Ali was having finding her next letter. After all, *R* was a very common letter. On *Wheel of Fortune*, *R* was almost always one of the first letters they picked. So why was she having so much trouble?

But I am not giving up.

Ali sat down on a bench in front of the student union and took a piece of paper out of her pocket. On the top she'd written an *R* in bright red marker, and under it was a long, *long* list of all the boy *R* names that she'd printed off a baby-naming web site. Ali knew it was a little silly, but she'd actually taken to carrying the list around with her for inspiration. She figured she'd have a better chance of finding her *R* if she went through the list and tried to get a clear picture in her head of a bunch of possible *R* guys. That way when she was walking around campus, she'd have a better idea who she should be keeping an eye out for.

Rudolph, Randall, Rupert. Rupert. *A Rupert would have shaggy brown hair, and all his clothes would be slightly too small. He probably smells like mayonnaise.*

Ali kept reading: *Rex. Rex always wears a helmet. And he carries a sword around with him wherever he goes. And he's hairy. Very,* very *hairy.*

Ralph, Ramone, Ramsey. Ramsey probably wears a lot of plaid, and maybe he has a Roman numeral after his last name.

Ranaldo, Reaves, Reilly, Reuben. A guy named Reuben would definitely have big muscles, or maybe he'd be sort of goth. No, wait, a guy named Raven would be a goth. . . . Ugh, this isn't getting me anywhere.

Ali crumpled up her paper and put it back in her pocket.

I just need one R. *Just one Reddington or River or Rumpel-fucking-stiltskin.* As far as Ali could tell, there had to be a near endless supply of boys with *R* names, so where the hell were they?

26

Later that night in the triple, Jodi completed step two. She called Will, aka Picks, and nervously listened to the phone ring once, twice, and then a third time. "What if I get his machine?" she whispered to Celeste with her hand over the mouthpiece, but then before Celeste could answer, Will picked up.

"Hello?" he said.

"Hi, Will?" Jodi breathed huskily into the phone.

"Yeah?"

Jodi was afraid to even look at Ali or Celeste, feeling like she would either crack up or throw up.

"This is Jodi," Jodi half whispered as if she were a professional phone sex operator and not a recently retired cabdriver.

"What do you want?" Will said.

Jodi paused. "You," she said. "I know it's crazy, but I can't stop thinking about how sexy it is the way you and Andrew are making us your—your *slaves*."

"Huh?" Will said, articulate as always.

"I love a guy who takes whatever he wants. It really, really turns me on. I mean, you know, I just love a guy who's cocky."

"Really?" Will said, sounding extremely skeptical.

"You know what else really, really turns me on?" Jodi whispered. God, she was a great actress. Maybe besides being in a hit band, she could be one of those crossover stars and act in some movies, too, like Madonna. "I mean, *really* turns me on, Will?"

"Uh, no. What?" Will asked.

"Kissing you," Jodi said.

"Who is this? Is this really Jodi?" Will asked. "Is this Nancy?"

"Well, I don't know who Nancy is, but I can prove that I really am Jodi. I'd love to prove it to you."

Jodi heard some noises in the background. "Wait, hold on a second," Will said. She heard muffled talking and two male voices.

". . . note . . . bitches . . . blow jobs . . . S and M . . . sexy . . . yeah!"

Will got back on the phone. He cleared his throat. "Okay," he said, deepening his voice in an obvious attempt to sound sexy. "So, uh, how do you intend to prove it?"

Jodi couldn't resist glimpsing at Ali and Celeste. Ali had her face buried in a pillow, and Celeste was sitting on the edge of her bed with her eyes as big as they could get.

Jodi almost faltered, but then she got control of herself.

"Meet me at the campus stables tonight at midnight," she cooed.

"Really? Uh, yeah. Okay," Will said.

"I promise I'll prove how turned on I can really get," Jodi said, wrinkling her nose as the words came out. "Oh, and Will, bring your friend Andrew with you. Ali thinks he's really cute." Out of the corner of her eye Jodi saw Ali making vomiting motions. She felt herself about to erupt with laughter, so she quickly hung up, then turned and gave Ali and Celeste high fives. It had totally worked. They were on.

27

Midnight came, and, wearing their sexiest outfits, Ali and Jodi showed up at the stables to find Will and Andrew already waiting for them.

"Well, look what we have here," Jodi said to Ali. "A couple of eager beavers."

"From what I understand, you two are the eager beavers," Andrew said.

"Andrew, please, we have some lovely ladies here—let's show them some respect." Will said, grinning evilly.

"No, no, Andrew's right. It's true, we are eager beavers," Jodi said instead of what she really wanted to say, which was, *Eeew.* "But it's not your respect we want tonight, boys."

"Really!" Will said.

Despite the unpleasant task at hand, it *was* a beautiful clear night, Jodi thought. It was really nice out by the stables. There weren't a lot of lit-up buildings around, so the sky shone with stars. The air was cold, but it felt great on her legs and back.

Ali looked really pretty in the moonlight. She had put on

this body lotion that had glitter in it, so her skin was all smooth and shimmery looking.

Jodi looked up at the sky for another moment, hoping that she would see a shooting star, but she didn't. She made a wish, anyway, though. That she and Ali and Celeste would always be friends. And that they would always feel as close as they did at this moment.

"So, aren't you guys going to do anything?" Ali asked.

Suddenly Will seemed dubious. "What are you two girls up to?" he asked.

"What do you mean?" Jodi asked. "We just like you, that's all."

Andrew nudged Will in the side. Will looked over, and Andrew made a bunch of rapid eye movements.[37]

"I don't know," Will said. "I think something's going on here." He started looking around, and for a couple of seconds Jodi and Ali worried that he would spot Celeste, Artha, and Jordan hiding a few yards away.

Jodi laughed. "There *is* something going on."

"What?" Andrew asked.

"Us. We're going on. I mean, we're turned on."

"You're not pulling anything?" Will asked.

"Well, we will if you want us to," Ali said.

Jodi gave Ali the planned signal, and each grabbed her guy and started passionately making out with him. Jodi and Ali went all out, really trying to be convincing.

□□□□□□□□□□□□□□□□□□□□□□□□□□□□

37 Universal guy sign language for—Man, we are possibly about to get laid here! Don't mess it up!

153

Jodi pressed herself up against Will, kissing his neck. Out of the corner of her eye she glimpsed Ali putting on a convincing show with Andrew.

In fact, Ali was already dragging Andrew into one of the empty stalls. Jodi picked up the pace a bit and started dragging Will into the stall next to them, keeping her lips locked to his the whole time.

"Okay," Ali said in a loud voice. "Now get naked."

"Yeah," Jodi said to Will. "I'd love it if you got, you know, totally nude for me."

While the guys were beginning to unbutton their shirts, Jodi and Ali got the handcuffs they had stashed under the hay.

Jodi dangled them in front of Will. "I was thinking I could use these to, you know, lead you into ecstasy," she said. She was really pretty damn good at this.

"Hey, where'd you get those?" Will asked, tensing up.

Oh, no, she thought. What if something went wrong?

"I brought these in my little evening bag," Jodi said, even though she and Ali hadn't been carrying purses. "Ali and I just thought it would be fun." She slowly started sliding the straps of her little sequined dress down over her shoulders and exposed a teeny bit of one breast. And with that the silly grin came right back onto his face.

Both Will and Andrew were practically slobbering, they were so excited. This whole thing was an absolute dream come true to them. Not only was this the single most exciting experience they'd ever had—two totally hot girls practically attacking them—but it would give them both jack-off material for, like, the rest of their lives.

"Thank you, God," Jodi heard Andrew say from the next stall.

Will and Andrew were now totally naked.

"Okay, let's see, why don't you stand over there," Jodi said to Will, pointing to a post that separated the stalls.

"Whoa," Will said, practically running to the post. He sat down with his back to the post and put his arms behind him, waiting for Jodi to handcuff him. "I knew you girls were kinky and slutty and all—but handcuffs? This is almost too good to be true." He sat back in the hay with his eyes glazed over.

Jodi heard Ali's cuffs lock shut around Andrew's wrists, and she quickly followed suit with Will.

"Oh, thank you, God," Jodi heard Andrew say again.

Jodi and Ali took a moment to stand back and admire their work.[38]

"Be right back!" Jodi said.

"Yeah, be right back!" Ali said.

They skipped out of the stalls to cries of "Huh?" and "Hey, where are you skanks going?" and into the night behind them.

38 Jodi and Ali would hate to admit it later, but both guys were pretty impressively endowed.

28

Celeste, Jordan, and Artha were waiting for Jodi and Ali right outside the stables.

"We did it," Jodi said.

"Yeah. It was great. Gross, but great," Ali said.

"Okay, so now, finally, the three of us get our turn," Jordan said. "Celeste and Artha and I were just dying to jump in there sooner."

"Well, it's good you didn't," Jodi said. "So far, everything has worked out perfectly."

Celeste checked her camera for the fiftieth time to make sure it was loaded with film and that the flash was working. Meanwhile Jordan and Artha stripped down to their boxer shorts.

"Okay, ready?" Celeste asked.

"Not quite yet," Artha said. "Jordan, your eyeliner is a little smudged." Artha helped Jordan with his eye makeup. They had put on lipstick and eyeliner for maximum effect. "Okay, now we're ready."

The five of them entered Will's stall.

His jaw dropped. "What are you doing?" he shrieked. He squirmed and squirmed, but there was no way to escape.

Artha and Jordan knelt down in the hay on either side of him and started snuggling him, pinching and tickling a little, too, while Celeste snapped away with her camera. "Oh my God," Celeste said. "I've already shot a whole roll of film. But luckily I have more!"

"Okay," Jodi said. "Let's have one with both boys standing over Will in their boxer shorts."

Jordan and Artha got into positions as if they were models and Jodi was the photo stylist.

"Yeah, that looks great," Jodi said, admiring her own handiwork. "Okay, for the next shot bend your knees a little more, guys. Great. Now give me naughty."

Click.

"Now ferocious, give me ferocious."

Click.

"Very good. You're beautiful, baby, beautiful."

Click.

Click.

Click.

"Hey, what's going on!" Andrew started shouting from his stall. "Tell me what's happening."

"Don't worry," Celeste said. "You'll find out soon enough. You'll get your turn."

"I'm sorry, man," Will called over the wall. "I wish I'd never found that fucking Filofax in the first place."

The Filofax? The one that Celeste had lost . . . the one where she'd been keeping track of all of their progress on the AHUL . . . the one she'd gotten back but had a weird feeling someone had gone through?

"THE FILOFAX!" Ali, Jodi, and Celeste all shouted in unison.

"So the mystery is finally solved, then," Celeste said thoughtfully.

"Yeah, after all this time. You know what the funny thing is?" Jodi said. "I don't really care all that much. I mean, we spent so much time wondering and now that we actually know . . ."

"Totally, dudes," Ali agreed. "This is just too much fun."

They finished with Will and proceeded to thoroughly humiliate Andrew, snapping pictures and totally making fun of him.

When it was all over, Jodi produced the key to the hand-cuffs and showed it to Will and Andrew. "Don't worry," she said. "We have the key."

She placed it just out of Will's reach.

"Yeah," Celeste said. "Don't worry about a thing. We'll put in an anonymous call to campus security, informing them of some kind of disgusting depraved gay orgy going on in the stables. And if you don't want these pictures leaking out, say, to the *Pollard Spectator* or even *The New York Times* . . ."

"Or the *Pollard Poofters*,"[39] Artha chimed in for the

39 The campus gay and lesbian newspaper.

hell of it. "Ooh, I like this headline—'Two Homophobes Come Out!'"

". . . then I'd advise you to leave us alone and keep your mouths shut about our list," Celeste continued.

And with that, they left.

29

They were practically ecstatic on the walk back to the triple. Jordan and Artha walked with them, and none of them could stop laughing as they relived every moment of what had just gone down.

"What could be better than that?" Ali asked.

"Nothing," Jodi agreed.

"I feel like such a weight has been lifted off my shoulders," Celeste said.

"Yeah," Ali said. "Now that this burden is off our chests, we can finally concentrate on other stuff. Like our new band!"

"Uh, excuse me, your new what?" Jordan asked.

"Our new band, The Lady Chatterleys!" Jodi said.

"The Lady Chatterleys?" Artha asked. "Who's in it?"

"Just the three of us, dude," Ali said.

"Well, dude, what about us?" Artha asked.

"Us who?" Jordan asked.

"Me and you," Artha told him. He turned back to Ali. "I play guitar, and Jordan is a brilliant pianist!"

"I'm a brilliant what?"

"Pianist. You can play keyboards."

"Artha, I think your hair mousse is leaking into your brain. I can barely play chopsticks. I mean, I can play some kids' songs I learned when I was little, like 'Twinkle, Twinkle, Little Star'—"

"I can play that one!" Celeste interrupted excitedly.

"And, you know, like, 'Yankee Doodle' and 'The Alphabet Song.'"

"What's 'The Alphabet Song'?" Jodi asked.

"You know—*a, b, c, d, e, f, g*," Jordan sang, hitting the notes with his fingers on an air piano in front of him. He cut to the end. "Now you know your ABCs, next time won't you sing with me."

"Hey," Celeste said. She'd just realized something bizarre. "That's the same tune as 'Twinkle, Twinkle'!"

"'The Alphabet Song?'" Ali said. "That's perfect for us. That could be our theme song, you know, 'cause of the AHUL. We should do the regular 'Twinkle, Twinkle' at the ceremony and then a super-jazzed-up rock remix of 'The Alphabet Song' at the reception."

"Are you on crack?" Jordan asked.

"Look, do you want to be in The Lady Chatterleys or not?" Ali asked.

"Definitely," Artha said. "I really can play guitar, you know."

"See?" Ali said to Jordan. "We'll actually have one person who knows how to play—so now you really have to join."

"Come on, Jordan, it will be fun," Celeste prodded.

"Okay, what do I have to do?" Jordan asked, shaking his head. "I mean, I thought what we did tonight was the craziest thing five college kids could do, but now you've found something crazier."

"All you have to do is show up for rehearsal tomorrow," Ali said. "Oh, yeah, and find an electric keyboard."

"So what do you say? Let's go out and celebrate," Artha said.

"I can't," Ali said before Jodi and Celeste had a chance to reply. "I have a paper to write about the themes of modern sexuality in the works of that dude D. H. Lawrence, and it's due on Monday. I absolutely have to work on it, and if I go out tonight to celebrate, I know I'll be all bleary-eyed tomorrow and I really want to be fresh. But you guys go."

"Excuse me? Could you please tell us what you did with our friend Ali?" Jodi asked, amazed.

"Yeah, come on, you've got to be kidding," Celeste agreed. She put her hand on Ali's forehead to see if she was running a fever. "You want to be fresh to write your paper instead of getting drunk with us?"

Ali sighed. "Dudes, this week has been pretty crazy, but I'm really digging that book. Celeste, you're the one always saying I have to buckle down and study."

Celeste nodded. "Well, yeah, but—I mean, you're actually *listening* to me."

"You're not mad, are you?" Ali asked.

"No, we understand," Jodi said. "And if you have to go

home and do work, then we'll *all* go home and do work."

"Yeah, as soon as the paper is finished, we can celebrate for real," Celeste said. "I'm actually pretty tired myself right now."

Jodi realized that she was, too. Humiliating two college boys was hard work! But finally, Jodi, Ali, and Celeste were all thinking, they could have a blissful, peaceful night of anxiety-free sleep. It was over. Andrew and Will wouldn't hurt them anymore, and they could go about their lives as if none of this had ever happened.

They yawned and hugged and said good night to Jordan and Artha Stewart. Then they went to their nice, cozy, comfy triple and went to sleep.

30

The next morning Jodi,[40] Ali, and Celeste all woke up to the phone ringing. They all just lay there at first, but Ali got up and answered it before the machine picked up. It was Ileana in a complete panic, her accent thicker than ever. She said it was absolutely imperative that she have her wedding that night.

"But how?" Ali asked. There was no way The Lady Chatterleys could do it that fast. They hadn't even had their first rehearsal yet!

"Please," Ileana begged. "You do it?"

"I'm sorry, but we really can't," Ali said. "The Lady Chatterleys have a prior, uh, booking."

"Is there some way? We really must have you at wedding," Ileana said.

"You've never even heard us play," Ali said.

"But you are only wedding band we know. Only band to reply to our flyer."

□□□□□□□□□□□□□□□□□□□□□□□□□□□□□□

40 Jodi had had an amazing sex dream involving Zack and that really cute guy from the first *Real World*.

"Can't you hire a DJ or something?"

"The money, we will make it doubled. A thousand dollars. And—and all free *booze* you can drink." The girl had certainly picked up that word fast.

"Uh, can you hold on a second?" Ali said. She covered the mouthpiece of the phone with her hand and whispered to Jodi and Celeste, who were now sitting up in bed listening to Ali's side of the conversation, "Dudes, she wants us to perform tonight for one thousand dollars. She's crazy."

Feeling newly empowered by the previous night's adventure, both Jodi and Celeste were totally gung ho. "Let's do it," they whispered back.

Ali went back to Ileana. "The Lady Chatterleys have suddenly become available," Ali said. "What? What kind of music do we play?"

She looked at her roommates imploringly for help.

"Standards," Jodi whispered. She had read enough wedding magazines in her life[41] to know that most brides preferred standards.

"Uh, standards," Ali said into the phone. "What? Oh, hold on a minute." She turned back to her friends. "What are standards, exactly?"

Jodi shrugged. Actually, she wasn't sure.

"It's like Cole Porter and Gershwin. You know, old stuff," Celeste whispered.

Well, that was good. "Twinkle, Twinkle, Little Star," "The

41 Sort of a hobby of hers.

Alphabet Song," and "Yankee Doodle" were certainly old songs.

"You know, old songs," Ali said into the phone. "Do we know any tunes by Type O Negative? Uh, yeah, I'm pretty sure we do. Okay, you want that to be your first song as husband and wife. And you want mostly punk and metal. Okay, no problem. Oh, but we only accept cash," Ali wisely added.

Ali grabbed a pad of paper and wrote down the details. They would play at the chapel "Here Comes the Bride" and all that and then head over to the reception immediately following at the frat house.

As soon as she got off the phone with Ileana, Ali called Artha and Jordan to tell them the news. They were totally into it. They arranged to meet in one of the music classrooms that day to rehearse.

"*Do* we know any songs by the band Type O Negative?" Celeste asked.

"Punk and metal?" Jodi asked.

"One thousand bucks and free booze," Ali answered. "It's too bad the groom's name doesn't start with *R*. I'm starting to think it's completely impossible to find an *R*. Isn't that the most ridiculous thing? There have got to be so many *R*s out there."

"But you can't kiss the groom anyway!" Jodi said. "Even if his name was Roger Robertson, you couldn't have kissed him. It's bad enough we're going to ruin their wedding by rampantly sucking as a band, but it would really make matters worse if you were to make out with the groom."

Crazier than going to Paris for Veterans Day weekend, crazier than trying to sell Jib's pot, crazier than what they had done to those two assholes the night before, even crazier than the Alphabetical Hookup List, agreeing to perform at Ileana and Melvin's wedding was the craziest thing they had done yet.

31

You know what they say—a terrible dress rehearsal means a good opening night. Well, Jodi, Ali, Celeste, Artha, and Jordan all certainly hoped that was true.

Needless to say, the rehearsal—if you could even deign to call it that—held in a practice room in PU's music building, was a complete disaster. For one thing, as Ali soon discovered, "Twinkle, Twinkle" is actually a very difficult song to sing on key. Also, it wasn't very long. Their first "set" ran about four minutes total. And they were supposed to play for at least four *hours*.

"That sounded terrible," Celeste said, untucking her borrowed violin from under her chin. Only Artha had produced something that could actually be called music.

"And it was so short," Jodi added.

"That's like that old joke," Ali said. "'This restaurant is awful—the food is terrible, and the portions are so small.'"

Nobody laughed.

That's when Ali reminded them that Ileana wanted a different kind of wedding. And metal and punk.

"What does that even mean?" Artha asked.

"I'm not sure," Ali said.

"Maybe we should just scream and bang around and make noises with our instruments," Jordan said. He was kidding, but it was actually a good idea. Or at least worth a try.

"You mean, like a haunted house or something?" Celeste asked.

"That's it!" Ali said. "I'll just scream and groan and moan, and you all play some weird shit, and we'll see how that sounds."

After they tried that for a while, they came up with plan B. Lip-syncing. They could do that toward the end of the evening when everyone was so loaded, they wouldn't notice.

"I'll go out and get a CD of that band they said they liked, Blood Types or whatever it was, and maybe a couple of other CDs, and I'll bring them to the gig tonight," Ali said.

"Wasn't it Type O Negative?" Jodi said.

"Dude, whatever, I'll get it and then we'll just lip-sync off it."

"But dude." Celeste giggled a little. She always giggled a little when she said the word *dude.* "We're not going to the wedding—we *are* the wedding. We're performing at it, remember?" she said, feeling exasperated. "Shouldn't we all get together before the wedding and memorize the words? I mean, how can we lip-sync if we don't even know the words?"

"Look, I have to work on my paper today," Ali said. "I can't spend the entire day on this. We'll be fine. We can wing it."

She had finished reading *Lady Chatterley's Lover* and was already in the middle of another book by D. H. Lawrence called *Women in Love.* (The really cute Spanish guy who had been working behind the desk at the library when she checked the book out that morning had punched her ID number into the computer and said, "Are you aware that every book you take out of the library is about sex?" "Of course I'm aware of that," she had said. They flirted for a few minutes, and even when it turned out his name was Enrique, she leaned over the counter and kissed him.) She really wanted to get some more schoolwork in before the gig.

"You know, I'm really looking forward to the wedding," Artha said. "Something different for a change."

"Are you saying what we did last night wasn't different enough?" Celeste asked.

"It'll be fun," Jordan said.

"I love weddings," Jodi said. "I can't wait." What she was really looking forward to was having an extra-great full-blown fantasy about walking down the aisle herself and seeing Zack waiting for her there—at least a seventy-pointer on her Zack Watchers points system—but of course she would never admit that, not even to her best friends. Some things were just too embarrassing to tell even them.

"So, then, we'll meet at the chapel with our instruments right before the wedding," Ali said.

"What should we wear?" Celeste asked.

"Oh God, I didn't even think of that," Ali said. "Do you dudes have tuxes?" she asked, turning to Artha and Jordan.

"Oh, yeah, sure, when I was packing for college, I figured I'd definitely need to pack a tux," Artha deadpanned.

"No need to be sarcastic," Ali said.

"I'm sure we can get a couple of tuxes from the costume department," Jordan put in.

"Great idea," Celeste said.

"Yeah," Ali agreed. "We should all do that. We should all go there and see what they have."

Just then there was a knock on the door. Ali opened it to find a disgruntled bassoon player with a beard who needed the room to practice in.

"What's your name?" Ali asked him, hoping it began with an *R*. If it did, she could agree to vacate the room in exchange for a kiss.

The guy gave her a funny look. "Uh, Devon?" he replied, making it sound like a question more than an answer.

"Oh," Ali sighed. "Oh, well." That was probably for the best, anyway, because his beard wasn't like a cool college-kid goatee beard. It was a full-blown, grown-up beard, like an insurance salesman would have.

"Why?" he asked.

"No reason," Ali said, moving aside to let him in.

The first official rehearsal of The Lady Chatterleys came to an end, and they all went their separate ways, agreeing to show up at the chapel and not to chicken out, no matter what.

32

Celeste was by far the most nervous. She was so sure that she would bomb with her violin that she stayed behind at the music building and asked Devon the bassoonist if he could help her at all.

"Well, let me hear you play something," he said, and Celeste launched nervously into her rendition of "Twinkle, Twinkle."

"Do you think you can you help me?" Celeste asked when she was done.

"I'm not Annie Sullivan," Devon said.

"Who?"

"You know, Annie Sullivan, Helen Keller's teacher. In other words, I'm not a *miracle worker*."

Actually, in a weird way, that was kind of funny.

"Come on," Celeste said. "I bet you're up to the challenge. You play the violin, too, don't you? Haven't I seen you around campus carrying a violin case?"

"Viola," he corrected. He acted like confusing a violin and a viola was the stupidest thing a person could do.

"Well, excuse me, *viola*," Celeste said. "But why don't you show me your stuff? On the bassoon, I mean, since you don't have your *viola* with you." She wasn't sure why she was suddenly being so brazen. Maybe she'd been through so many humiliating things recently that this seemed like nothing.

Devon stared at her for a moment, his eyebrows furrowed, then finally began playing scales on his bassoon. "That sounds beautiful," Celeste said.

"Really?" Devon looked at her and paused, as if he were waiting for her to make some kind of sarcastic remark—sort of like the one he'd just made to her.

"Yeah. I mean, you have total control over your instrument,[42] I can tell," Celeste said.

"Yeah, that's kind of true, I kind of do have total control over my bassoon," he said, looking down at his bassoon lovingly. He removed his reed and shook some spit out of it. The spit made a tiny heart-shaped puddle on the classroom floor.

"I wish I could do that," Celeste said.

"Well, I *have* been playing for a really long time," Devon said, sounding happy but just a little embarrassed. "I guess I could give you a few pointers for the violin. If you're still interested."

Celeste smiled. "Thanks. I'd really appreciate it. So, where should we start?"

Devon reached out his hand and very tentatively took hers. He brought it up to his face, and for a second Celeste thought that he was going to kiss it.

---

42 Ali or Jodi would have *never* been able to say this line with a straight face.

"First off, you should probably trim your fingernails. If they're too long, you can't properly position your hand on the fingerboard and most of your notes will be either sharp or flat. Luckily I always keep a little nail clipper in my bag because you never know when you're . . ." Devon looked down at his hand, which was still holding her hand, and started to blush. "Um." He let go, went to his backpack, and took out a tiny silver clipper and handed it to her.

Celeste went over to the trash can. For some reason, she couldn't stop blushing. She'd never realized how personal cutting one's nails could be.

After she'd finished, they both sort of stood there quietly. Then Devon cleared his throat.

"So, uh, why don't you try playing a scale for me?" he offered.

Celeste plodded through a very off-key C scale.

"Argh. That was really bad, wasn't it?" Celeste asked.

"Well," Devon said. "Your tone wasn't too terrible. I think it was just that the notes were a little . . . Here, let me show you."

Devon took the violin and played. The way he played it, it didn't just sound like a scale, it sounded like a whole song. He handed her back the violin. "Now you try."

She positioned her hand on the strings.

"No, see," he said, "your fingers need to be closer together." He reached out and gently pushed two of her fingers together.

Suddenly Celeste remembered something. "Kissing cousins!" she said excitedly.

"Huh?" Devon said.

"Kissing cousins. It's this thing my violin teacher used to say when I took a few lessons a long time ago. I'd be playing and she'd say, 'Kissing cousins,' and it was supposed to remind me to put my fingers closer together."

"That's pretty weird," Devon said.

"I never really thought about it before, but in retrospect, yeah, I guess it kind of is."

Devon laughed. "Well, so long as it helps you stay in tune."

Celeste played the scale again, and this time it didn't even sound so bad.

After a few hours, more of what she used to know came back to her (which admittedly wasn't all that much, but it was better than nothing).

At the end of the day, when he was standing behind her, supporting her bow and correcting her form, Celeste suddenly felt overwhelmed with gratitude. She turned around and—already in his arms—kissed Devon on the lips. He was taken aback at first and sort of froze for a moment, but then he gently kissed her back. He, of course, was used to a thin wooden reed between his lips—not Celeste's tongue.

"Thank you, Devon," Celeste whispered. "Oh my God," she said, noticing the big white clock on the wall. "Now I've got to get to the costume department."

"You're like Cinderella and I'm like your fairy godmother," Devon said. "No, wait, that didn't come out right."

Celeste was already out the door when she realized that Devon had just called himself a fairy godmother. She stopped and laughed. In a weird way, that was pretty funny, too.

33

Jodi was the first to arrive at the chapel. It was so beautiful. Why hadn't she ever come here before? She hadn't even bothered to see it on any of her campus tours. Being Jewish, she had always figured, what did she need with the chapel? But it was so peaceful and relaxing just being there.

She put her trumpet down on the organ bench, which was off to the side of the altar, and sat in the first row of benches or pews or whatever they were called. She looked all around at the stained glass windows, which had beautiful scenes of angels doing stuff, and at the wall of brass plates with the names of all the rich PU alumni who had donated money.

She wondered if she would one day be rich and donate money to PU. It was kind of a funny thought, considering she hadn't even paid her library fines yet. What would she be like at her ten-year Pollard reunion? Would she be married? Would she have a baby? A real career?

Everything was already so different from what she had imagined. When she'd arrived at PU after her long drive there with Buster, she'd thought she and Buster would be together forever. She had really thought they would be married as soon as they graduated. Maybe they would have even gotten married here, on campus, in this chapel. Jodi shuddered. Thank God she hadn't married Buster. She'd been saved. She couldn't even imagine marrying Buster now. He probably would have showed up for the wedding wearing his T-shirt with the picture of Pac-Man and the words *Eat Me* written on it.

Since she was sitting in a sort of a church or whatever, she figured she might as well pray. She closed her eyes. "Thank you," she whispered. *For saving me from Buster,* she thought. *For giving me such great roommates. For everything.* "Thank you," she whispered again.

"You're welcome, dude," Ali said, sliding into the pew next to her.

Jodi jumped, nearly knocking into the pew in front of her. Ali had really startled the shit out of her. Jodi knew it wasn't God talking, calling her "dude," but still, it was weird.

"What are you wearing that for?" Ali asked, staring at Jodi's tuxedo, complete with bow tie, and sounding extremely dismayed.

"What do you mean?" Jodi asked, staring at Ali's black gown, which was sort of reminiscent of the twenties, replete with sequins and fringe. "What are *you* wearing *that* for?"

"I said we should go to the costume department and find outfits," Ali said.

"I did," Jodi said. "You said we should all get tuxedos! I thought we all agreed to wear tuxes, remember?"

"No, I don't remember," Ali said. "I said Jordan and Artha should wear tuxes, but *we* should *obviously* wear formal dresses. We're not The Gentlemen Chatterleys, are we? No, dude! We're The Lady Chatterleys."

"You mean Celeste's not wearing a tux?" Jodi said, finally catching on.

"Of course not!" Ali said.

"So I'm the only one wearing a tux?" Jodi was starting to panic a little.

"No, you're not the only one wearing one. But you are the only girl wearing one," Ali said, which wasn't exactly comforting.

Now Jodi felt like a complete dork. The tux was too big on her, and she had cuffed up the sleeves about five times, and the bow tie was a lopsided clip-on. Plus the thing was waiter quality at best. The material was stiff and scratchy, and the crotch of the pants hung down too low. She looked terrible. But there was no time to do anything about it. Guests were already beginning to arrive, and ushers wearing suits were escorting them down the aisle to their seats.

"What if I see someone I know?" Jodi said. Of course, she was thinking of Zack in particular, but she didn't want to admit it.

"Just act like you meant to wear it," Ali said. "It really doesn't look that bad."

That was when Jodi noticed that one of the ushers was Nanjeeb, her disgusting ex-boyfriend Buster's roommate. That was strange. Jodi couldn't imagine Nanjeeb having any friends beside Buster, because he was antisocial and nerdy and always talking about how things were better back in his country.

"What are you doing here?" Jodi asked Nanjeeb.

"What are *you* doing here?" Nanjeeb asked. He looked at her outfit. "The caterers are supposed to be at the reception place."

"You're an usher?" Jodi asked, ignoring his caterer comment.

"No, I am not an usher!" Nanjeeb said. "Is that some kind of racial slur? You think because I am Indian, I must work as an usher in a movie theater or something? If you must know, I happen to be the best man."

"Really!" Jodi said. "Where are the groom's parents?"

"They wouldn't come," Nanjeeb said. "They don't approve of this union."

"And what about the bride's parents?" she asked.

"Not possible. Do you know how much it costs to fly in from Transylvania?"

"Wait. Huh? What are you talking about?"

This whole thing was getting more and more bizarre. For one thing, all of the other guests were students at PU. There were no other family members present, just kids wearing jeans and T-shirts. And for another thing, there were really weird decorations lining the aisle. Okay, it wasn't bizarre to have ribbons tied into big bows at the end of every row of pews, but it was a little odd to have a skull and crossbones in the center of every bow and for the bows to be black. What kind of wedding was this, anyway?

34

Jodi and Ali walked over to the organ, where Celeste, Artha, and Jordan had already gathered.

Great, Jodi thought. Celeste was wearing a stunning blue strapless gown with a slit up the back that fit her perfectly, and Jordan and Artha were wearing much nicer tuxedos than she was. Theirs had nice crisp white shirts and fancy cummerbunds, silk bow ties, and cuff links.

"I'm so nervous, I think I'm going to throw up," Celeste said.

"You look great," Ali reassured her.

"Yeah, you really do," Artha said. "That dress is stunning on you. And Ali, you look like the most gorgeous dude here."

"Thanks!" Ali said, swinging her hips from side to side a little to make her fringe move.

"I'm sorry, sir," Artha said to Jodi. "We must have the wrong room. Judging by your suit, I'd say we have accidentally stumbled upon your bar mitzvah. So sorry."

"It's not my bar mitzvah." Jodi pouted. "I thought we were all supposed to . . . Oh, never mind."

"There's no sign of Melvin or Ileana," Ali said, looking around the chapel nervously.

"Good, maybe they won't show up and the wedding will be called off," Celeste said. She shakily ran her bow over a string by way of a warm-up.

But it didn't look like that was going to happen, because a guy—actually a midget of some kind, who seemed to be the minister—appeared from the rectory and stood in front of the altar, facing the weird congregation.

He indicated to The Lady Chatterleys that they should begin.

Jordan took a seat at the organ, but he didn't play. He laid his electric keyboard on top of it, which luckily had some prerecorded pieces in it that you could set to different beats like samba, meringue, rap, and waltz. One of the prerecordings was a very somber-sounding processional piece, and he flicked the switch so it would play. It came out really soft, so he turned the volume way up, but nobody seemed to notice the band at all. They were all turned around in their seats with their necks craning all over the place, waiting to see the bride walk down the aisle.

Jodi turned to look with the rest of them and didn't even notice the groom as he came out of the rectory and took his place at the altar beside Nanjeeb.

First the ushers walked down the aisle, each with a bridesmaid on his arm. The bridesmaids wore long black velvet gowns, and each held a single long-stemmed red rose. They were obviously trying to keep from sticking themselves with the thorns that no one had bothered to remove.

Finally it was time for the bride to make her journey down the aisle.

Jordan gave the signal, and the Lady Chatterleys began their special version of "Twinkle, Twinkle," with Celeste leading on the violin.

Twinkle, twinkle, little star . . .

The bride appeared in a long white velvet gown. In lieu of a veil she wore a white velvet cape with a hood and dolman sleeves. She carried a bouquet of black roses. Under the pointy white velvet hood of her cape, Jodi saw her face. It was Gothina. It was El Gothra. It was Count Gothula. It was Gothenstein.

How I wonder what you are . . .

It was Buster's girlfriend.

Did Buster know about this? Ali had said that the bride's name was Ileana and the groom's name was, what?

Up above the world so high . . .

Melvin! That was Buster's real name. Buster was just a nickname.

The groom was Buster! Buster was getting married.

Like a diamond in the sky . . .

Jodi turned her head to the altar, and there, standing in front of the midget, was Buster, wearing a new white T-shirt that said Lick My Ween and Suck My Peen on it in big black letters. Holy shit! Jodi was sort of hyperventilating. *Okay, okay,* she thought. *Jodi, think, it's just Buster. You don't care about him anymore.*

Twinkle, twinkle, little star . . .

Still, it was weird having your ex-boyfriend get married while you were wearing a hideous ill-fitting tuxedo and totally forgetting to play the trumpet you were holding in your hand.

How I wonder what you are . . .

She looked to Ali and Celeste for help, but they were both totally oblivious to the fact that they were playing at her ex-boyfriend's wedding to the freak of the century. Jesus, didn't the words *rebound girlfriend* mean anything to anyone? You weren't supposed to marry the first person you dated after a long relationship like the one she'd had with Buster. Everybody knew that! And why couldn't Ali and Celeste stop concentrating so hard on singing and playing the violin for a second so she could get their attention?

Finally the song ended, and The Lady Chatterleys put down their instruments so the ceremony could begin. And that's when Ali and Celeste noticed the groom. Their eyes widened and they looked at Jodi, horrified.

"I didn't know," Ali whispered.

Celeste swallowed hard as a wave of nausea came over her. Buster wasn't exactly someone she wanted to watch getting married any more than Jodi did. After all, she had made a terrible mistake and lost her virginity to Buster, and even though he had already broken up with Jodi, Jodi had of course been incredibly upset and had refused to speak to Celeste for weeks over it.

"If anyone here knows any reason why these two should not be joined in holy wedlock, speak now or forever hold your peace," the midget said.

Jodi needed to get Ali and Celeste alone for a minute to discuss this.

She watched the bride and groom exchange vows and silver skull rings.

"Then by the power vested in me over the Internet, I now pronounce you . . ."

It was at that moment that Celeste threw up.

She made a loud retching noise, and the whole congregation looked over at her, totally disgusted. Celeste's violin case was filled with puke, and Celeste was staring down at it in shock like a street musician who had just been given a ten-dollar bill.

Jodi grabbed Celeste's hand and Ali's arm and dragged them out of the chapel and onto the lawn.

35

The first thing they did when they got outside was to help Celeste sit down on the grass.

"Are you okay, Celeste?" Jodi asked.

"Yeah," Celeste said weakly. "Jodi, are *you* okay?"

"I think I'm in shock," Jodi said.

"Jodi, I'm so sorry," Ali said. "I had no idea Ileana was Buster's girlfriend, and I had no idea that Melvin was Buster."

"I know," Jodi said. "It's not your fault."

"I can't believe he's already getting married," Celeste said. "I mean, it seems like he's totally on the rebound."

"Maybe she's pregnant or something. She did suddenly seem in an awful hurry for this wedding to happen. But anyway, I'm sure they're not really in love," Ali offered.

"I guess it doesn't really matter," Jodi said, slightly unconvincingly. "I mean, it's not like I care that much about Buster anymore. It's just a little weird that he's, you know, getting married."[43]

☐☐☐☐☐☐☐☐☐☐☐☐☐☐☐☐☐☐☐☐☐☐☐☐☐☐☐☐

43 No matter how over a guy you are, it's always weird to find out he has a new girlfriend. It's even weirder to find out he's getting married.

"Actually, I think he *is* married," Ali corrected, slightly unhelpfully.

"And it's also weird to find out like this," Jodi said. "You know, finding out *at* the wedding."

"Oh, Jodi, it's awful," Celeste said, gathering her strength and giving her a hug.

"It *is* awful," Ali said. "I almost fainted when I saw him standing there."

"What should we do?" Celeste asked.

"I don't know," Jodi said.

"Should we just run away?" Ali asked. "I could buy us all beers at Dimers and we could forget this ever happened."

"Ugh, don't say the word *beer*," Celeste said, putting her hands on her stomach.

"Well, should we go back in there and finish the wedding?" Ali asked.

"I don't know," Jodi said.

"It's up to you, Jodi," Ali said. "Celeste and I will do whatever you want. I'll even put on your tux and give you my dress if it will make you feel better."

Suddenly the whole thing seemed hilarious to Jodi. Absolutely screamingly funny. She burst into hysterical laughter, bending over and holding her sides.

Ali and Celeste thought she was crying.

"It's all going to be okay," Ali said.

"Yes, Jodi, please, please, don't cry," Celeste said.

Finally Jodi was able to stop laughing long enough to

speak. "I'm not crying, I'm laughing. This is fucking hilarious!" she said, gasping for breath.

Ali and Celeste looked at each other and started laughing, too.

"So, what should we do?" Ali asked.

"We're going to go back in there and do what The Lady Chatterleys do best," Jodi said. "We're going to suck!"

"Yeah!" Ali said. "Huh?"

"We're going to suck so bad, they'll beg us to stop!"

"But then we won't get paid," Celeste said.

"So? We'll consider it a little wedding gift to the happy couple," Jodi said, wiping laugh tears from her eyes.

Just at that moment the blushing bride and the extremely intoxicated groom rushed out of the chapel, followed by rice-tossing throngs of college kids. They began their raucous parade across campus to the frat house where the reception was being held.

A very confused Jordan and Artha spotted Jodi, Ali, and Celeste and came running over to them. "What the hell's going on?" Artha asked.

Celeste brought them up to speed.

"So we're going to go through with it?" Jordan asked.

"It's show biz, baby," she said. "The show must go on. The Lady Chatterleys never quit a gig."

36

When The Lady Chatterleys arrived at the "reception" at Beta Phi House, they were horrified to find everyone already drunk on keg beer and the bride and groom dry humping on the makeshift living-room dance floor while everyone cheered them on.

"Go, Buster, go, Buster, go, Buster."

It was like a *Ricki Lake* wedding.

They had taken the "garter ceremony" a few steps too far, and Buster had managed to remove the bride's panties and was twirling them over his head.

All the "single men," which was literally *all* the men, gathered together to catch Ileana's panties. Jodi couldn't help watching their pathetic display. She smiled at one loser's valiant effort to get the panties, which led to a couple of bloody noses. She was just about to turn away and help the others set up their "equipment" when she noticed some-one familiar in the crowd of guys. No way. It couldn't be.

It was.

Zack.

Jodi's mouth dropped open. What the hell was Zack doing here? Somehow Zack standing there with the Beta Phi boys was even more astoundingly shocking than Buster standing at the altar with Ileana. This was too much! Zack was always going on and on about how much he hated these places.

Jodi shook her head. She had to get out of here. This horrible, horrible day had to end. And why exactly hadn't she taken Ali up on the offer to trade clothing?

As soon as Artha finished setting up the mike so the Lady Chatterleys could begin "playing" or whatever it was they were going to do, the frat president, a red-faced jarhead named Eddie, grabbed the mike and started slobbering into it.

"Excuse me, ladies and germs," he said. "I have to make a speech, I mean, a toast, I mean, a roast." He burped loudly into the microphone. "No, that's not the toast. As you all know, our brother Buster can no longer live in our house and be one of us. A Beta Phi must be single, no old ladies around."

Eeew, Jodi thought. Old ladies? Who talked like that?

Eddie continued. "So, our brother Buster will have to leave us." Eddie turned toward Buster and put his hand over his heart. "But Buster, man," he said in a sentimental voice. "We will totally invite you back for all the ragin' keggers. And now that you're loaded, we'll even let you pay. Heh heh heh."

Now that you're loaded? Jodi blinked. Since when was Buster loaded?

"Pay this, bitch!" Buster yelled from his seat, sticking up his middle finger.

"And so," Eddie continued. "We've decided to induct another man to the Beta Phi brotherhood in your place."

Hushed whispers shot around the room.

"So now please raise your glasses, or actually your plastic cups, to honorary brother Zachary Greenspan!"

"To Brother Zachary," everyone cheered.

Now Jodi *really* felt like she was about to pass out. This was all too weird. Was she dreaming? What was it you were supposed to do again to make sure you weren't dreaming? Oh, right, you were supposed to—

Ow. Okay, definitely awake.

Zack went up to the mike and thanked everyone for this "honor," promised not to hog the bathroom, and suggested everyone start a round of "keg laps" on the lawn. "Chug, chug, chug!" he chanted.

"Chug, chug, chug," everyone chanted back.

Jodi couldn't believe what she was hearing. So if she wasn't dreaming, was she maybe hallucinating? Had she just entered bizarro world? Was this a joke?

Maybe this whole night was a joke. Were they doing some kind of remake of that old show *Candid Camera*? Was this some kind of real-world torture show and she was the unknown victim? Maybe she'd win something like a trip to Hawaii. This had to be a setup—first Buster getting married to Gothzilla and then Zack joining this cult of slobs.

She marched forward and pulled Zack aside.

"I think you have some explaining to do," she snarled.

"I think *you* have some explaining to do," he said.

"Me? Why?"

"What's with the cross-dressing?" He looked her up and down and then condescendingly adjusted her clip-on bow tie.

Jodi pushed his hands away. "Are you actually a member of this fraternity? What about all that stuff you always said about individuality and nonconformity and sowing the seeds of revolution?" She was practically screaming.

Zack just shrugged sheepishly.

"What about living on a goddamned kibbutz in Israel? Is this your idea of a fucking kibbutz? What about what you said about the poetry of the people? Chug, chug, chug—is that your idea of the poetry of the people?"

"I never said anything about poetry of the people," Zack protested.

"Well, you definitely said sowing the seeds of revolution. Is this your revolution?" She gestured toward the crowd. "You're a regular Paul fucking Revere!"

"Well, then maybe you'll kiss me, that is, if you're up to *P* on your sick little list." He sounded really nasty.

Jodi was absolutely furious. "I can't believe you have the nerve to throw that in my face when *you're* the biggest hypocrite in the world. You're no better than any of these other animals." Buster was lying on his back while two guys dragged him around by his feet. "I can't believe I ever liked you." She threw up her hands in disgust and exasperation, turned from him, and walked away.

The Lady Chatterleys were about to begin playing, but they were having technical difficulties. Ali had sort of fucked up the lip-sync tapes. They were all set to pretend to play "Girls Just Want to Have Fun" when the tape started and it turned out to be an old French language tape of Ali's. *"Ferme la porte,"* a man's voice said slowly. "Now, repeat after me. *Ferme la porte.* Close the door."

"I thought I had taped over that," Ali whispered.

Jodi grabbed the mike. "I'm going to sing a song," she announced.

"Jodi, what are you doing?" Celeste whispered, trying to get the mike away from her.

But it was too late. Jodi launched into a venomous solo a cappella performance of "Idiot Wind," by Bob Dylan, Zack's favorite musician. Everyone stopped what they were doing and just stared at the insane girl in the tux.

When it was over, she turned to her band members. "How was I?" she asked.

Celeste stepped forward. "You were . . ." Terrible, atrocious, totally off-key. "Passionate and interesting," Celeste said.

Zack carefully approached her. "Jodi, may I speak to you for a minute?"

"What do you want?" she asked, not realizing that she had said it into the mike.

"Please come outside and talk to me for a minute," Zack said.

"Fine." Jodi handed the mike to Ali and followed him outside to the veranda.

"Look, Jodi, I *had* to rush this frat. I mean, come on, I desperately needed better housing. The rooms in this house are at least twice the size of my dorm room, and I share my room with that crazy racist asshole, but here I could have my own room. Plus the radiator in my room has been broken all year and nobody's bothered to fix it, no matter how many times I've filled out those fucking maintenance reports. It's like fucking *a hundred degrees* in there all the time. What was I supposed to do?"

But no matter how much he rambled on, Jodi just shook her head. He was full of crap. She didn't have to wait to get to *Z* to kiss him, she just needed to get to *H* for hypocrite, which was totally what he was.

"Well, I hope you'll be very happy in your new home," she said, and turned to leave.

As she was walking back into the frat house she ran into Ali, who was walking out with a big grin on her face.

"Where are you going?" Jodi asked.

"Home," Ali said.

"But The Lady Chatterleys must go on," Jodi said, hiking up her baggy tuxedo pants.

Ali held up five one-hundred-dollar bills. "While you were out there talking to Zack, we played our special version of 'The Alphabet Song' and Ileana agreed to pay us half the money as long as we promised not to play any more for the rest of the night. Five hundred bucks for sucking!"

"That's great," Jodi said. But she was more interested in the all-you-can-drink part of the deal, anyway. "So I guess that's why you're smiling like you just got a present from the Easter bunny?"

"Well, that and one more thing—I got my *R*! Some guy named Reggie who actually wore a *name tag* to the party. You know, those 'Hi, my name is' deals? I can't believe it—here I've been struggling this whole time, and then it just falls into my lap."

Jodi tried to force a congratulatory smile, but her heart wasn't really in it after the fight with Zack. "So, wow, you're down to eight letters," she said. "But hey, you're really not even going to stay for one drink?"

"Nah," Ali said. "I've accomplished a lot for one night. I've got too much work to do at home to move on to *S* tonight."

Jodi looked at her in disbelief. Was she a bad judge of character or were people just never what they seemed? Buster, the cheater from hell, was suddenly getting married as a freshman in college. Zack, who she'd thought was the most sincere person in the world, was a hypocrite, and Ali was the only student on campus studying on a Saturday night.

Where was Celeste?[44] At least she could depend on Celeste to be her same old reliable, innocent, sweet virginal self.

□□□□□□□□□□□□□□□□□□□□□□□□□□□□□□□□

44 Making out!

37

Once Ileana had called them off stage and Celeste had set her violin beside its puke-filled case, she was overwhelmed with an incredible relief. All of her feelings of sickness disappeared, along with all the anxiety and tension of the last twenty-four hours.

Once she had taken this acting class where you had to perform these different sensations, and she'd had to act out feeling like she was walking on clouds. That's how she felt at that moment, but she wasn't acting.

Well, except she could stand to feel a little bit fresher after the whole throwing-up incident and everything. But that was easy to solve.

She went upstairs to find a bathroom, then once she found one, she squeezed out about half a tube of Crest and brushed her teeth with her finger. There were paper cups and a bottle of Scope with a bar shot pourer on top of the sink, and she filled a cup and gargled. Once she was done, she splashed some cold water on her face.

Then she looked at herself in the medicine chest mirror. She looked pretty with droplets of water on her lashes. In fact, she thought, in that blue strapless gown, she could honestly say she had never looked better.

She was going to leave when she suddenly thought, *Maybe I should stay.* It was a party, after all. And she was all dressed up. Why was she always rushing off someplace? Why shouldn't she stay and at least see if she could have fun?

She went back downstairs and looked around the frat living room. And that's when she saw them—Will and Andrew, aka Picks and Elbows—sitting in the corner, drinking. They looked totally miserable, as if they were drowning their humiliation of the previous night in booze.

Elbows looked up and caught her eye for a moment and then quickly looked down at his drink. He looked *scared.* This was so great! He was too scared even to look at her.

And it was there, standing on the Beta Phi stairs, that Celeste had an epiphany. What better way to drive home her victory than to get herself back into the AHUL here and now? She could do it right in front of these two jerks. She could kiss every guy in the room if she wanted to, and they would know what she was doing, and they'd be too scared to say anything to her or to anyone. It would just remain their little secret.

Celeste had a strange feeling of power. She had a new and as yet untapped self-confidence. She was not just going to *play* the AHUL, she was going to win—and without cheating. Although Darius had turned out not to be a real *D,* she had gotten another *D*—Devon the bassoon player! Even if she hadn't thought of it as her *D* at the time, she had kissed him, and it counted. So it was going to be *E* through *Z*, and it was going to be all in one night!

"Ha," she said out loud, in the direction of Picks and Elbows. "Hooray for me from *E* to *Z*."

Celeste walked up to Eddie. "Hello, Mr. Frat President," she said in a sexy Marilyn Monroe voice.

"Hello!" Eddie said, looking down at her cleavage.

"I've always wanted to, you know, do it with the president. Just call me Monica Lewinsky," Celeste said, putting her arms around Eddie's fat neck. She spotted a guy she knew named Frankie over Eddie's shoulder. He would be her next victim.

"Well, okay, Monica," Eddie said, laughing. He thought he was the funniest guy in the world.

Who cared? He was an *E!* Celeste kissed him passionately for the time it took for her to sing 'The Alphabet Song' from *A* to *Z*,[45] the whole time keeping her eye on Frankie and an RA named George who had just walked in.

□□□□□□□□□□□□□□□□□□□□□□□□□□□□□□

45 That's the official length of time a kiss has to take as per rule #1 of the Official AHUL Amendments.

38

When Jodi walked back into the frat and saw Celeste standing in the middle of the room totally making out with disgusting Eddie, she just couldn't take it. It was like the whole world as she knew it was coming to an end.

She decided the thing to do was to call it a night and just get into bed. She grabbed a bottle of something that was wrapped in a fancy silver Mylar bag from the windowsill and read the card. *To the new Mr. and Mrs. Buster, congratufuckinglations! The Wigman.*

"Thanks, Wigman," Jodi said to no one, and headed home.

When she got back to the triple, Ali was sitting at her desk, writing furiously. She looked downright manic. Jodi frowned, confused. Then she noticed the empty box of No-Doz that sat on Ali's desk next to her books.

Jodi opened the Wigman's wedding gift—a bottle of Jameson's—and crawled into bed with it, swigging dramatically from the bottle.

Ali was so absorbed in her work, she didn't even look up.

Jodi took another swig and it went down the wrong way and she almost died, choking as loudly as she could and practically falling out of bed.

"What's the problem?" Ali finally asked.

"It's over for good between me and Zack," Jodi explained. "I mean, he's not even who I thought he was. He's just as big a jerk as anyone, bigger, and I don't even care about him anymore. I completely misjudged him."

"It's probably all for the best," Ali said. Then she launched into a caffeine-fueled diatribe. "The problem with self-righteous dudes like Zack who are all up on their high horses all the time—and you know I'm speaking from experience because Sensei[46] was the exact same way, always talking all this shit about how he was going to change society and save the world—is that they're so caught up in their own scenes and ideals and egos that they can't see the forest for the trees, and if they just stood back and took a good long look in the mirror. . . . Actually, what am I saying? That's all these fucking narcissistic dudes do is look in the mirror. If they would just stop and step away from the mirror for five minutes and look at the world around them, they would see that there are actually other actors in their movie, you know, and that your voice is not just their personal fucking sound track, I mean . . ."

Jodi tuned her out after about the first thirty seconds. She appreciated that Ali was trying to make her feel better, but it wasn't helping. Because, Jodi thought, this was the

□□□□□□□□□□□□□□□□□□□□□□□□□□□□□□□□
46 Ali's boyfriend in the very beginning of book 1. He went to NYU and dumped her via cell phone.

thing, the fact of the matter, the truth: She was still very much attracted to Zack. And this was the question, the problem, the big fucking mystery of the universe: Why did she only seem to fall for assholes?

Okay, maybe it wasn't the nicest thing to do to Ali, but Jodi took a few more gulps of Jameson's,[47] lay back on her bed, and did like lazy-eyed, narcoleptic K. J. Martin and passed out. Or at least pretended to.

Ali finished her rant. "Jodi? Jodi?" she said.

But Jodi didn't answer, and thankfully, Ali forgot all about Sensei and went back to typing furiously.

---

47 Jodi's note to self: *If I ever get married, remember to serve Jameson's.*

39

Celeste had started a new list on a personalized napkin embossed with the words *The Wedding of Ileana and Melvin*. In between kisses she marked down each new name next to its corresponding letter, right in full view of Elbows and Picks.

A—*Andy the Bloated*

B—*Buster*

C—*Junior Security Officer Craig Brown*

D—*Devon***

E—*Eddie**

F—*Frankie**

G—*George*****

H—*Hilliard**

I—*Irv***

J—*Jesse****

K—*Kegger (He swore that was his name and everyone called him that)**

L—Louis***
M—Marco (Hottie)*****
N—

Celeste was drunk, and as she looked proudly at her list she realized that she didn't even remember some of these people. For instance, *I* and *J* were just a fog of blurry lips. Let's just say she wouldn't be able to pick these guys out of a police lineup. Also, she was sort of vague on the whole new starring system (each guy earned between zero and five stars) she had come up with. She wasn't exactly sure what her scoring criteria were—she just let her lips be the judge. She was definitely having a fantastic night.

Now she was up to *N,* and what do you know, Nanjeeb was right there! Unfortunately he was trying to break-dance, which he just shouldn't have been doing. His dress shoes looked like enormous planes trying to take off on a runway and then crashing.

Celeste stood over him. He had lowered himself to the floor and was trying to balance on one hand and slowly move his big feet in a clunky circle.

Finally he stood up. "Ow," he said. "I must remember never to do that move again. I have carpal tunnel syndrome."

Probably from jerking off, Celeste thought. And then she thought, *Eeew.* What had come over her? She was like a totally different person.

Anyway, she was wasting time. She had to get to *Z* by

sun-up. She wrapped her arms around him and smooched him right in the middle of the dance floor.

Nanjeeb pushed her away. "Unhand me, you tramp!"

"Shorry," she slurred. She suddenly felt really bad.

"First you pass out in my room in the bed of Buster while I am trying to sleep—"

"I'm sorry about that, too," Celeste said. She cringed, thinking about that horrible night. How could she have had sex in Buster's bed when Nanjeeb was right in the next bed, just a few feet away? That was so disgusting. Of course, a lot of kids on campus did that, since it wasn't exactly like they could check into the Four Seasons Hotel—they really had no choice—but still, it was so disgusting. And it had been her first time, which made it so much worse. Nanjeeb had *watched* her lose her virginity.

"I'm sorry about what happened that time when I was in the room with Buster," Celeste said. "It was extremely rude of me."

Nanjeeb scowled at her. "Well, I don't know. I swear to my God, combine that with this sacrilegious green-card marriage of Buster's and I am almost ready to transfer myself right out of this place."

Huh? "Nanjeeb, what are you talking about? What green-card?"

"Buster and Mrs. Buster have a sham marriage. Mrs. Buster's mother and father paid Buster to marry her so that she would not be sent back to Romania."

"Wow," Celeste said, her mouth dropping open. *I can't wait to tell Jodi!* "Well, anyway, I really am sorry I had sex in your room right there in front of you. Really. I truly aplogize."

Nanjeeb narrowed his eyes in confusion. "You didn't have sex in my room," he said. "Don't you even know when you have sex?"

"What?" Celeste said. She was totally confused. "What do you mean?"

"You didn't have sex. You were too drunk to do anything but pass out. Buster took off your clothes, then passed out himself. And I had to witness this disgusting display of immorality!"

Celeste stood there in shock. She couldn't believe what she was hearing. She wasn't surprised that Buster's marriage was a fraud, but the fact that she was still a virgin was the most fabulous, mind-blowing, amazing news she could ever have heard. She was still herself. An overwhelming feeling of relief coursed through her body.

She could still choose who she would have sex with for the first time. It would be a beautiful decision, not a drunken mistake. It would be someone she liked or, actually, someone she loved. Buster hadn't taken that away from her.

Just then Buster stumbled by, smoking a disgusting fat cigar. Just the sight of him made Celeste sick. He was so out of it, he hadn't even noticed that The Lady Chatterleys consisted of Jodi, Ali, and Celeste. And he didn't seem to notice that his bride was passed out cold in an overstuffed chair and that someone had drawn a mustache on her and written *Property of Buster* on her forehead.

Celeste immediately marched over to Buster and slapped him as hard as she could across the face.[48]

☐☐☐☐☐☐☐☐☐☐☐☐☐☐☐☐☐☐☐☐☐☐☐☐☐☐☐

48 This can be a very dramatic, effective, and extremely feminine gesture, but one must be drunk to perform it correctly.

Buster put his hand to his stinging cheek as everyone in the whole fraternity started laughing at him.

"What the hell was that for?" Buster asked.

"That was for Jodi," Celeste said.

Then she slapped him again.

"And *that* was for purposely making me think that I had slept with you."

40

Dawn came, and Jodi hadn't slept—not even for one tiny minute. Thoughts of Zack, combined with Ali's incessant tap-tapping at her keyboard, had kept her wide awake.

Ali sat back in her chair. "I have just completed the greatest single college essay in the history of We-We-Western civilization." All that caffeine had made her stutter a bit. "Can I read it to you?"

"I don't know," Jodi said. "How long is it?"

"Twenty-four pages," Ali announced.

"Maybe in a little while," Jodi said.

"Dude, let me at least read you this one paragraph," Ali insisted. She started reading, but Jodi couldn't concentrate. She just kept replaying the events of last night over and over again.

There was an awkward moment of silence. "That was great!" Jodi said, trying to sound as convincing as possible. "I think I'm going to take a shower," she added quickly before Ali had a chance to read any more.

Jodi grabbed her towel and locked herself in the bathroom. She stood under the hot shower for a long time.

Maybe she shouldn't have berated Zack like that.

But then she had this totally bizarro memory. She remembered this time when her family had first gotten their dog, Kookla. When he was a puppy, he had this disgusting habit of eating other dogs' shit. Jodi's father would scream at the dog, "Stop eating shit, Kookla! Do you want to be a shit-eater all your life?" It was a really strange thing to remember, she had been so young at the time, but it just kept coming into her mind. And then she realized that she, Jodi, no longer wanted to eat shit. She had a right to be treated well. She had a right to have her opinions and not take shit from Zack. She had done the right thing to confront him, although maybe she could have been a little nicer about it.

She brushed her teeth and blow-dried her hair and thought maybe she'd go for a run, but when she went back into the room, she did her favorite thing instead—she got back under the covers wet and wrapped in a towel. And she felt a lot better for some reason.

But something didn't feel quite right. Jodi's eyes traveled around the room. Ali, Ali's desk, Celeste's empty bed, the clock. Wait a second. Jodi focused in on the clock. It was 6 A.M. and Celeste wasn't back. She hadn't been home *all night.*

"Ali?" Jodi sat up, still hugging the comforter around her. "Don't you think it's weird that Celeste isn't home yet?"

Ali looked at her and shrugged. "It's not that late. What is it, like two o'clock? Three?"

"Well, you're right about one thing. It's not *late* anymore. It's early. Look, the sun is already up."

"Huh? No, it's not. I mean, I know I had a lot of caffeine, but I can't have been sitting here *that* long." Ali looked out the window. "Oh, crap. Dude, I've been sitting here all night. Where *is* Celeste?"

"I don't know," Jodi said. "She never stays out late."

Ali started pacing. "Do you think there's a chance—"

"A chance of what?" Jodi asked.

"Nothing," Ali said.

"What!" Jodi said, getting upset.

"Well, what if Elbows and Picks did something to her? I mean, maybe we went too far with them. You know, the whole gay thing."

"You mean, maybe they were so ashamed by the threat of homosexuality that they found her and chopped her into tiny little bits or something?" Jodi said. "Oh my God." She was suddenly totally freaked out. She had no idea what to do.

They went back and forth for a few minutes in a sort of a panic, deciding exactly what to do, and finally decided they should go search for her. They were about to get dressed when the door flew open. In walked Celeste in her blue strapless gown.

She could barely stand up. "I have a man with me!" she said.

Jodi and Ali looked at each other.

"I hope you're decent," Celeste said, the word *decent* throwing her into a fit of giggles.

Jodi and Ali laughed, relieved to see her standing there in one piece.

"Who's the dude?" Ali asked.

"Oh, just some hottie I picked up," Celeste said, hiccuping.

She went to the door and grabbed the guy, dragged him in, and hung all over him. Jodi's eyes bugged out of her head. It was Zack!

Jodi leapt out of bed. She was totally aghast. Of all the low-down, despicable things anybody had ever done. . . . She opened her mouth to speak, but nothing came out. She felt like she was going to explode.

"I . . . I . . . ," Jodi said.

"I won!" Celeste blurted out.

Jodi and Ali stared at her.

Celeste hiccuped.

"Well, okay, I didn't get *X*—but that's pretty much impossible. So I skipped over it and went right to *Y*. Look."

She handed Jodi three crumpled-up napkins. Jodi smoothed one of them out and looked at it.

"What does it say?" Ali asked.

"It says, 'The Wedding of Ileana and Melvin,'" Jodi said, totally freaked out and extremely annoyed.

"No, look at the other side. It's my list. *A* to—"

"Where's *Z*?" Ali asked, snatching the napkins out of Jodi's hand. "You've got Quentin, Reggie—hey, I kissed him too!—Sam, Tito, Uncle John . . . Uncle John?"

"Will's uncle," Celeste said ecstatically. "The one who

works for *The New York Times.* He was on campus visiting his darling nephew, so I made sure to get him on my list."

Ali continued reading from the napkin. "Vance, Wigman, Yasuo, and hey, you didn't win—there's no *Z*."

"Well, that's what I've been trying to say. I've been working on *Z* now for like *four* hours, but the guy just won't kiss me!" Celeste giggled and gave Zack a big squeeze. "He says he's in love! He's a one-man woman! I mean . . ."

And with that she slumped back into Zack's arms. Zack carried her over to her bed and laid her down.

Jodi swallowed. "What did Celeste mean by that?" she asked.

Zack walked over to the stricken Jodi and grabbed her hand, while Jodi held on to the towel she was wrapped in with the other hand.

"She means," Zack said, "that I've been a jerk. The more I thought about it, the more I realized I was letting my ego get in the way of what I really wanted. You were totally right, everything you said at the party. If I can bend my ideals for nicer accommodations, then why can't I do it to be with someone I can't seem to get out of my head?" He stopped, blushing. "I got all bent out of shape over a harmless little kissing game that held no more significance than spin the bottle," he continued. "A game that, frankly, just made me *jealous.*"

Jodi started to smile.

"I have to admit, though," Zack added, "I needed some help getting over myself. It was only after four hours of

Celeste telling me what an idiot I've been that I finally realized she was right. That both of you were right. First, I'd like you to know that I'm stone-cold sober. And second, Jodi, I think I'm in love with you."

Jodi had no idea what to say. She just started crying, wiping her eyes with the towel while at the same time trying to keep herself covered up. She'd never imagined she could feel so overjoyed.

"Well, dude, don't just stand there!" Ali yelled. "Kiss him, for God's sake."

Jodi and Zack kissed, and every single bad feeling of the past few weeks melted away, as if being absorbed into her blue terry-cloth Martha Stewart towel. But before the kiss got too hot and heavy, Jodi stepped back for a moment. A thought had occurred to her.

"Zack? Can I ask you something? A favor for a friend?"

Zack laughed. "Anything," he said.

Jodi pointed to Celeste, passed out on the bed.

"I want you to kiss Celeste on the lips for the amount of time it takes to sing the alphabet song in your head. That way she'll win fair and square and the game will be over once and for all."

"Wait a minute," Ali said. "I'm not so sure. What about *X*? I mean, I've kissed two *X*s in my life and Celeste just skipped over it."

"But *X* is really hard," Zack said, coming to Celeste's defense. "I mean, I don't know any guys whose name starts with *X*."

Jodi looked admiringly at Zack. It was so sweet of him,

not just to be so understanding, but to actually help them with their game. "There's probably not one single guy on campus whose name starts with *X*."

"Hey, maybe you're right," Ali said. She went to her computer, logged on to the school's student database, and opened the student roster. She did a first-name search for all names that start with *X*, and *your search returned 0 results* popped up on her screen. "You're right," Ali admitted. "There isn't one *X* name at Pollard. Not a single one. PU is *X*-less. So Celeste really *did* win!"

"You mean, she *will* have won, once Zack does the honors," Jodi corrected. "It's up to him."

Zack laughed and shrugged. "I feel so powerful," he said. "So *needed*. I just hope I'm up to the challenge." Then he bent over Celeste and kissed her very tenderly while Jodi and Ali burst into uproarious applause.

41

Celeste woke up that evening feeling like she'd been run over by a bulldozer. She opened her eyes very slowly to see a much too cheerful Jodi and Ali standing over her, grinning. Ali handed her a thick coffee milk shake with a bendy straw, but Celeste was too weak to hold it, so Jodi just sort of leaned it against her.

Celeste managed to lift it to her head and use it as an ice pack.

"Oh, God," she moaned. "Please don't tell me I did anything stupid."

"Hmmm," Ali said. "Stupid? No, actually, you were brilliant."

"I don't suppose you'd call *winning* the Alphabetical Hookup List stupid?" Jodi said.

Celeste opened her eyes fast this time, which hurt. "What?" she asked.

"You won," Jodi and Ali said at the exact same time.

"You have to be kidding. Ha ha," Celeste said weakly.

"You won," they said again.

"I *won?*" Celeste asked. "I don't even *remember.*"

Ali and Jodi laughed and handed her the proof—her napkins. Celeste looked at them in disbelief. "What the hell are all those stars?" she asked.

"We were going to ask you the same question," Ali said.

Celeste blinked groggily, then narrowed her eyes at the name *Nanjeeb* as a fuzzy memory started to come back to her.

"Guys, wait," she blurted. "I—I think . . ." She trailed off, trying to call back the exact conversation or at least the closest thing possible. "I'm still a virgin!" she exclaimed. Ali and Jodi exchanged confused looks.

"Dude, I'm sorry, but it kinda doesn't work that way," Ali said. "You can't really revirginate yourself just by finishing the list."

Celeste started to laugh and didn't even pay attention to the throbbing pain it caused in the back of her head. "No, you don't understand—Nanjeeb told me last night that I didn't really sleep with Buster that time. I just got to their room and passed out, and Buster made me think we'd had sex, but we didn't." Celeste beamed at Jodi. "And oh, there's more—Buster only married that girl so she could stay in the country. Her parents paid him. The marriage is all a fraud."[49]

Jodi laughed. "That's no surprise," she said. "I guess that's what the frat guy meant about him suddenly being loaded."

□□□□□□□□□□□□□□□□□□□□□□□□□□□□□□□□□□□□

49 Ileana's parents promised to pay Buster five million Romanian leu if he agreed to marry her. When he found out that five million leu equals roughly $150.09, he was really angry. "Even that crappy band got paid more than me!" is what he said to Ileana later. Then she promised to buy him an I'm a Lesbian Trapped in a Man's Body T-shirt and the *Girls Gone Wild Best of Spring Break* video, and he promptly forgave her.

"But isn't this great? I mean, not only am I still a virgin, but I didn't have sex with your ex-boyfriend, either. So I'm not a lousy friend after all."

"Well, you did make out with Jodi's boyfriend last night," Ali pointed out.

Celeste closed her eyes and groaned. "No, Jodi, please, I didn't know . . . Zack? *Z!* Oh, God . . ."

"It's okay, Celeste," Jodi reassured her. "It's totally okay."

And it was okay. Jodi lay on her bed reading *Southern Bride* and happily, unguiltily thinking about Zack as much as she wanted—no more Zack Watchers points for her. Now she could binge on Zack all she wanted. Ali spell-checked her D. H. Lawrence paper about fifty times. And Celeste quietly nursed her hangover while it slowly sank in that she had won. Won! And that everything had worked out perfectly, and all was well and intact, including her virginity. Oh, and by the way, did she mention that she WON!

42

The next weekend the girls were in their room, getting ready to go out. Celeste wore her blue strapless gown, Ali wore her fringe number,[50] and Jodi forwent the tux and dressed like a girl, too, in a gorgeous black off-the-shoulder dress.

A car honked. It was their ride, a surprise from Jodi.

"Okay, is everyone ready?" Jodi asked.

"We're ready," Celeste said.

Jodi went to the door and opened it, and there was lazy-eyed, narcoleptic K. J. Martin, just stopping by to see if she and Hallie could have a party in their room.

"Wow, you girls look amazing," LENKJM said. "Where are you going?"

"Oh, we're just going out celebrating," Ali said. "It's a party for Celeste."

"Is it your birthday or something?" LENKJM asked Celeste.

□□□□□□□□□□□□□□□□□□□□□□□□□□□

50 They are in big trouble with the costume department for obvious reasons.

"No, it's not her birthday—we're celebrating a certain accomplishment."

"Well, do tell," LENKJM said. "Can I go with you?"

The three girls looked at each other. If there was one thing they had learned in their time so far at PU, it was that K. J. would soon fall asleep. "Um, why don't you come in and sit down," Celeste said. She gestured invitingly to her bed.

"Well, uh, okay," lazy-eyed, narcoleptic K. J. Martin said, coming in and sitting down on Celeste's bed. Within seconds she was sound asleep and Jodi, Ali, and Celeste tiptoed out of the triple and down the stairs.

Celeste and Ali were amazed to see a black stretch limo waiting for them outside. It was totally scratched up and dilapidated, but it was still a limo. An enormous black woman got out of the driver's seat and opened the back door for them.

Celeste felt like a princess. She slid into the limo, followed by Ali. "Thanks, Dakota," Jodi said before she got in. "It's incredibly nice of you to do this for free. I really owe you one."

"My pleasure, Love Bug," Dakota said.

She drove them to Zuppa Alphabeta, a swank, trendy Italian restaurant on Peachtree Street in Buckhead, the most fun neighborhood in Atlanta. Of course, Jodi had chosen it based on the name. It was Jodi and Ali's treat as promised. After dinner they could do whatever Celeste wanted—go to Mako's, or the Tongue & Groove, or this English-type pub called the Rose and Crown, or a great place Ali had heard of called the Have a Nice Day Café. They could barhop in Virginia-Highland, another nice Atlanta neighborhood, or go to this amazing alternative rock club called the Cotton Club and listen to music. Or they could just have Dakota drive them around town in luxury.

Jodi had made sure Dakota stocked the limo with a cold bottle of champagne, but she forgot the glasses. Jodi opened the bottle, anyway, and they all took swigs, laughing and toasting.

When they were almost there, some conversation started coming in over Dakota's radio in the front seat.

"I'm sorry, Love Bugs, I can't turn this thing off," she said.

She tried to press the button to raise the glass partition between the front of the limo and the back so the girls could have privacy, but that was busted, too.

"It doesn't matter," Celeste said.

Suddenly some low, deep moaning came in over the radio.

"What's that?" Ali asked.

"I don't know," Dakota said, completely baffled. "I'm just the dispatcher. I haven't been behind the wheel in years."

"Oh, baby, yes, yes, there, oh, yes, right there," sounded over the radio.

Then another voice responded. It was a man's voice. "Oh, Pia, baby, you're the best," he said.

"What!" Dakota screamed. "She's cheating on me! And with a *man!*" She said the word *man* like it was some kind of terrible disease. "Well, she's one dead Love Bug!"

43

When Jodi, Ali, and Celeste arrived at the restaurant, they found a bottle of wine waiting for them at their table. There was a note attached by a ribbon that said, *Dear Celeste, Congratulations! Your Friend, Zack.*

The maitre d' opened the wine and poured them each a glass while Jodi flushed with happiness.

"To Celeste," Jodi said, raising her glass.

"To Celeste, the winner," Ali said.

Celeste's eyes welled up with tears.

"What is it?" Jodi asked.

"I'm just really happy, that's all," Celeste said.

They clinked glasses and tasted the delicious wine.

"Well, it's not Paris," Jodi said.

"It's better than Paris," Ali said. "It's home."

"Let's drink to that, too," Celeste said.

"Actually, I have something else we can drink to," Ali said. "My English professor loved my essay on D. H. Lawrence so much, he's putting it up for a special PU award."

"Ali, that's great!" Jodi said.

Celeste jumped out of her chair and hugged her. "Who would have thought you'd be the scholar of the bunch!" she said.

They all laughed.

"But then again, who would have thought I'd win the Alphabetical Hookup List?" Celeste added.

"And that I would end up with Zack?" Jodi put in.

"Dude, I think we all *knew* you'd end up with Zack," Ali said.

"To the Alphabetical Hookup List," Celeste said, initiating yet another toast.

"To the Alphabetical Hookup List!"

The waiter came over then to take their order. "Good evening," he said. "My name is Xavier, and I'll be your waiter."

Jodi, Ali, and Celeste looked at each other and burst out laughing. "Is it too late?" Celeste whispered.

Ali raised her eyebrows, then glanced back up at the waiter. "Dude," she said. "I think you'll be a lot more than just our waiter."[51]

□□□□□□□□□□□□□□□□□□□□□□□□□□□□□□□□□□□□□□

51 This is the end of the book, dude.

The Alphabetical Hookup List

An all-new series

A–J
K-Q
R-Z

Three sizzling new titles from
PHOEBE McPHEE
and MTV Books

www.mtv.com

www.alloy.com

Like this is the only one...

Floating
Robin Troy

The Perks of Being a Wallflower
Stephen Chbosky

The Fuck-up
Arthur Nersesian

Dreamworld
Jane Goldman

Fake Liar Cheat
Tod Goldberg

Pieces
edited by Stephen Chbosky

Dogrun
Arthur Nersesian

Brave New Girl
Louisa Luna

The Foreigner
Meg Castaldo

Tunnel Vision
Keith Lowe

Number Six Fumbles
Rachel Solar-Tuttle

Crooked
Louisa Luna

Don't Sleep with Your Drummer
Jen Sincero

More from the young, the hip,
and the up-and-coming.
Brought to you by MTV Books.